THE
AWAKENING
OF
KUNDALINI

THE
AWAKENING
OF
KUNDALINI

Gopi Krishna

A Dutton   *Paperback*

E. P. DUTTON NEW YORK

LIBRARY OF CONGRESS CATALOGING IN PUBLICATION DATA

Gopi Krishna, 1903–
The awakening of Kundalini.

1. Kundalini. 2. Meditation. 3. Yoga. I. Title.
BL1215.K8G66 1975   294.5'4'3   74–28323

Published under the auspices of the Kundalini Research Foundation,
New York, New York 10016.

10 9 8 7 6 5 4 3

Published simultaneously in Canada by Clarke, Irwin & Company
Limited, Toronto and Vancouver
ISBN: 0-525-47398-X

Contents

Introduction   vii

I What Everyone Should Know
About Higher Consciousness   1

II The Ancient Concept of Kundalini   9

III Is Meditation Always Beneficial?   40

IV The Goal of Meditation   62

V The True Aim of Yoga   77

VI The Dangers of Partial Awareness:
Comments on Alan Watts' Autobiography   96

VII An Interview with Gopi Krishna:
On Mystical Experience, Drugs,
and the Evolutionary Processes   106

Introduction

In *The Awakening of Kundalini* the author writes from his own direct experience of enlightenment, the supreme goal of all spiritual disciplines, including meditation. This is a book for everyone who wishes to know the basic facts about meditation and the energies that it can set in motion.

Gopi Krishna was born in the small village of Gairoo, in Kashmir, the northernmost state of India. There, where the fabled Vale of Kashmir and its Mogul gardens nestle high in the Himalayas, the author has lived nearly all of his seventy-two years. They were difficult years from the very beginning. Unable to continue his education beyond high school, he entered government service and worked as a minor official until his retirement.

A number of years ago, he founded the Research Institute for Kundalini at Nishat, outside the capital city of Srinagar, where he resides, and he now devotes all his time to research.

The Indian government is also taking up a Kundalini research project in an attempt to verify the claims of ancient adepts.

In his investigations, Gopi Krishna has found that during recent times there have been very few instances of individuals in whom the serpent fire burned ceaselessly from the day of its awakening until the last, bringing about mental transformations known to the ancient sages of India. Gopi Krishna awakened the serpent fire in himself in December, 1937, at the age of thirty-four, after seventeen years of almost daily meditation. He would concentrate intently on a spot above his eyebrows for approximately three hours each morning before leaving for his office. Of the event that occurred on this particular morning he wrote: *

> Suddenly, with a roar like that of a waterfall, I felt a stream of liquid gold entering my brain through the spinal cord. The illumination grew brighter and brighter, the roaring louder . . . I [became] a vast circle of consciousness in which the body was but a point, bathed in light and in a state of exaltation and happiness impossible to describe.

This experience, the duration of which he could not judge, marked the beginning of a total transformation in consciousness that has since become a permanent feature of his being. It is because of this, and because of the documentary research he has carried on for many years, that he now writes about a subject and enunciates a doctrine that, save for some veiled hints in a number of recondite ancient esoteric documents, is being presented for the first time in the form of a workable field theory, covering all psychic and spiritual phenomena.

From what he has experienced and continues to experience whenever he chooses to direct his attention inward, Gopi Krishna is led to the conclusion that the universe we see is only one of the facets of a creation that is hidden from our sight. In another dimension of consciousness other facets come into view that are so surprising and so surpassing that what

* *Kundalini, the Evolutionary Energy In Man*, Shambhala Publications, Berkeley, 1970.

we observe with our normal consciousness is reduced to insignificance. This is the reason why mystical experience has always been indescribable. The term "Neti, Neti," meant "It is not this, nor is it that; it is simply indescribable!" What they experienced in the state of Cosmic Consciousness could not be described because it was from another dimension altogether.

Though this is true, Gopi Krishna is frequently asked to describe his experiences in this other dimension, and he has attempted to do this in several works already published and in the process of publication, particularly in *The Riddle of Consciousness.*

Not long after his initial awakening of the Kundalini force that December morning, he wrote that he had felt then like a small child venturing outdoors for the first time and finding himself on the shore of a billowy ocean, utterly lost between the two worlds in which he lived—"the incomprehensible and infinitely marvelous universe within and the colossal but familiar world without." He went on to say, in his autobiography, *Kundalini, the Evolutionary Energy in Man:*

> When I look within I am lifted beyond the confines of time and space, in tune with a majestic, all-conscious existence, which mocks at fear and laughs at death, compared to which seas and mountains, suns and planets, appear no more than flimsy rack riding across a blazing sky; an existence which is in all and yet absolutely removed from everything, an endless inexpressible wonder that can only be experienced and not described.
>
> As the result of a day-to-day observable but still incomprehensible activity of a radiant kind of vital energy, there has developed in me a new channel of communication, a higher sense through which I am able on occasions to have a fleeting glimpse of the mighty, indescribable world to which I really belong—as a slender beam of light, slanting into a dark room, does not belong to the room which it illuminates, but to the effulgent sun millions and millions of miles away. . . . I perceive a reality before which all that I treat as real appears unsubstantial and shadowy, a reality more solid than

myself, surrounded by the mind and ego, more solid than all
I can conceive of including solidity itself.

In his writings, Gopi Krishna is not adhering to any ancient
or modern metaphysical system. He believes that the intellect
alone cannot solve the riddle of creation, but that through the
process of gradual evolution, humanity will come into possession of other faculties and other means of perception to gain
knowledge of what are at the moment completely hidden, all-
pervasive energies and forces. With this enhancement in his
mental faculties, man will be able to draw a more accurate picture of the cosmos, which is necessary for the understanding of
the ultimate.

The idea of human consciousness transcending the limitations of the senses and entering into a nonmaterial world is
something unimaginable. For the religious-minded, the thought
that mystical experience is the foretaste of a higher state of
consciousness, toward which humankind is evolving, is at first
sight unacceptable, for it shatters our dream-world of God and
soul, sin and virtue, bondage and emancipation, and many
other concepts common to the religions of the world.

But then Gopi Krishna has always been conscious of the
difficulties he faces in winning acceptance for such a novel and
unexpected idea. The concept of prana—that "radiant kind of
vital energy"—for instance, has not yet entered the thinking
of psychologists and scientists of the West, though discoveries
of new elementary particles that do not fit into the framework
of their present knowledge may force such a breakthrough in
the future. In discussing consciousness and mind, we are dealing with entities that cannot be defined in terms of the properties ascribed to matter, such as size, texture, grain, weight, etc.
Mind and matter might be derivatives of the same basic substance, but the properties of the two are poles apart.

Our sensual equipment, therefore, cannot apprehend consciousness, and we can never know through it what happens in
another mind. How then does a living organism function? How
does thought or an act of will influence the body cells? There

must be a connecting link between the two. To hold, as some modern biologists do, that body and mind are inseparable, would be to reduce consciousness to an epiphenomenon and to deny an independent existence to life and consciousness. To hold that consciousness is the sole reality and the visible world an illusion creates other difficulties.

Gopi Krishna's task is to bring the physiological bridge, leading to higher states of consciousness, to the attention of open-minded scientists and intelligent laymen for investigation. Though a vast volume of literature exists at present about human evolution, the biological organ responsible for it has remained a mystery. From the religious side no explanation has been offered so far about the mystical trance and the religious experience. Gopi Krishna's disclosures about Kundalini thus provide, for the first time, a bridge between religion and science.

Once the existence of the bridge is proved and accepted, thousands of seekers, drawn from all over the world, will train themselves for the supreme condition he describes in these and other writings. Those who succeed in this enterprise will investigate the metaphysical implications of their experience, thus laying a foundation for the science of consciousness. For the enterprise of Yoga, of which meditation is but one branch, is not intended merely to procure peace of mind or a vision of God, or psychic gifts. Rather, it is designed to raise the aspirant to the lofty stature of an intellectual prodigy and prophet.

It is only the genuine prophet or enlightened man or woman who can lay his finger unerringly on the causes responsible for the world crises we face. True revelation, reaching far beyond the current values and tastes of a certain period in history, draws attention to the prevailing errors in thought and faults in conduct inimical to the progress of mankind. It reaffirms faith in divine guidance and presents to the intellect new concepts and ideas that are not or are only dimly perceived by it.

Gopi Krishna has no inhibitions against cooperating with any scientist or institute where dissemination of Truth is the aim. He urges scientists the world over to investigate the physiological bridge to higher consciousness with the same dedication and urgency that characterized the Manhattan Project of the 1940s and resulted in the invention of the atom bomb.

He is not a guru, nor does he want followers. He has no illusion and no pride that the wisdom of the earth is concentrated in him. For he knows very well that after investigating and studying for aeons, man will have drunk only a few drops from the Infinite Ocean that feeds the universe. Gopi Krishna will gladly help in making known any hidden gem of truth wherever it is found, but it must be a universal truth to help all humanity.

The only possible way for the race to survive lies in a psychological revolution, establishing the primacy of spirit over flesh in a manner that meets the demands of modern science and satisfies the present-day intellect. This would be the empirical verification of a psychosomatic law that is acting behind all spiritual and supernormal phenomena witnessed in history. He believes—as he wrote some time ago—that this is but a short distance in the future:

> In but a decade, at the utmost two,
> The world of science shall have found the clue
> To that mysterious chamber of the brain,
> Which healthy meditation tends to train,
> To flood with radiant psychic energy,
> Drawn from the ambrosial reproductive tree,
> And then, illumined by a wondrous light,
> It brings the hidden world of Life in sight.

Gene Kieffer
November 24, 1974

THE
AWAKENING
OF
KUNDALINI

I

What Everyone Should Know About Higher Consciousness

It is often hard to convince a man about the error in his own thinking. If it were easy, there wouldn't be so many different points of view, each convinced about its own authenticity, justified by argument. There wouldn't be so many different schools of philosophy, or such a variety of political ideologies.

It is common to see people defending their opinions and beliefs even when palpably absurd and untenable. But the mind exhibiting the untenable view is so possessed or warped that, try as we might, it is not possible to dislodge it from its stand. This is why we see such a vast diversity of opinions on the issue of higher consciousness in hundreds of books, each representing a different point of view.

From this it is easy to imagine the colossal nature of the task of anyone who sets out to prove that it is possible for an individual to exceed the limits of human consciousness. For in this plane of reality, the observing mind and the objective world assume a different relationship; not as the subject and the object, but as the two aspects of one underlying reality.

There is an obvious difficulty in presenting an idea entirely new and beyond the comprehension of an ordinary mind. This concept is so far removed from our normal experience that it is extremely difficult for anyone to accept readily without falling prey to doubts and uncertainties.

It is because of this difficulty and behavior of the mind that one of the most persistent phenomena in history, resulting in cataclysmic changes in human thought, still remains a mystery. At best, it is a controversial issue among intellectual leaders, and its implications for the future of mankind have been completely obscured.

I refer to the appearance of great mystics, seers, and prophets, including Christ and Buddha, on the stage of history.

The upheavals they caused in the thoughts and lives of countless people—with their glimpses of a higher realm of creation, their own example, and their exhortations for a nobler life—are interwoven with the whole fabric of history.

Can we ascribe all of the ferment they caused, and the faith of millions they commanded for hundreds of years, merely to a chance occurrence or a delusion of the multitudes? If not, have we ever come close to understanding the mystery lying behind their births and careers? What force drew them to prodigious acts of renunciation and martyrdom? What power spoke the inspired phrases that were to become household words and stir the hearts of people even today? What magnetic power allowed them to gain such a hold on their disciples and followers, so that their names are still alive in the hearts of countless people? Even from this great distance, these prophets dwarf eminent thinkers and intellectuals who rose after them.

The world has been so carried away by erroneous descriptions of higher consciousness presented in modern times, that it has completely shut out the fact that the most outstanding examples of transhuman consciousness—the great mystics and founders of religions—both in their mental stature and mode of life evidenced certain extraordinary characteristics that are absolutely beyond the territory of altered states of consciousness induced by drugs, biofeedback, hypnosis, or autosuggestive meditation techniques.

All these methods produce only ordinary men and women. Some may be prone to visionary experiences, clairvoyant insights, or even to creative flashes, but ordinary all the same. None are even remotely comparable to these outstanding figures of the past.

Many individuals today claim to have achieved the highest state of consciousness, but it would take pages to list their names. We can begin with familiar writers such as Ram Dass [he has often claimed to have reached Samadhi, both with drugs and without] and John Lilly, who says the same in the introduction to his book, *Center of the Cyclone*. Then there are many mystics, Masters, Gurus and Saints, hailing from India, Tibet, the Middle East and other places, who all claim to be in the state of Super Consciousness or Cosmic Consciousness. All of these advocate different techniques, but none discusses the biological aspects or the evolutionary processes.

The validity of psychic phenomena is widely admitted even by some scientists, though no one is able to assign a plausible reason for it. Some scientists are even prepared to accept the credibility of bizarre phenomena, like that produced by Uri Geller and others. Dr. Andrija Puharich ascribes some of Geller's extraordinary feats to the mental influence of extraterrestrial beings. Equally fantastic explanations are often given for the weird occurrences witnessed at mediumistic séances.

There is perhaps no realm of knowledge that provides such a vast field for the exercise of the phantasmic faculty in man as the occult and the paranormal. But it is not readily accepted that the power behind the extraordinary performances of spiritual geniuses and the force behind psychic phenomena are both the outflow of a springhead of intelligent energy, present in the human organism. The explanation, though simple and rational, free of any fantastic overtones, is shunned.

What I am asserting, with a full sense of responsibility, and based on my own experience, is that there is a marvelous potential present in the human body that is drawing humankind toward a sublime state of consciousness inconceivable for even the most intelligent mind that has not experienced it.

The appearance of all extraordinary prophets and mystics of the past—most of whom were credited with psychic faculties —and the existence of outstanding mediums and sensitives, are historical facts. They provide irrefutable evidence for the fact that the human brain has a capacity for extraordinary manifestations that we have not as yet been able either to understand or explain.

The issue remaining to be explored and authenticated is the existence of the potentiality, present in the human organism, to create this extraordinary condition of the brain. And for this purpose, scientific investigation into the phenomenon of Kundalini can provide the necessary avenue.

That man is evolving toward a state of awareness in which the reality behind the universe can become perceptible is entirely beyond the dreams of our most far-seeing intellects. What this investigation will establish in full—corroborated by hundreds of ancient esoteric books from India, China, and elsewhere—is the startling fact that the activity of the reproductive mechanism can be reversed; and the precious energy, instead of flowing downward and outward, can stream inward and upward.

This reversal, true for both men and women, causes an amazing transformation in the cerebrospinal system, leading to an explosion in consciousness. It is difficult to describe adequately the sense of infinitude and immortality brought about by this transformation.

Let us suppose that the reproductive apparatus, by reacting upon itself—using its own concentrated vital energy—is able to enhance its activity many times more than what exists in normal men and women. This highly increased aggregate of genital secretions and essences, then, is used to rebuild the nervous system and the brain.

It is the same when these vital organs are built up in a fetus in the womb, as the elementary particles of nature are drawn from every part of the body, according to biological laws not yet understood. But now the reproductive system is employed as a transfer center, where these life-energies are transformed into an even more volatile or radiant energy that streams upward into the brain, producing paranormal states of consciousness and psychic activity.

With this enormous flow of the most powerful nerve energy into the brain, continually for years and years, the horizon of the mind can be extended to a degree that is entirely beyond the capacity of a normal brain. This transformation is built on the copiously produced ambrosia of the reproductive mechanism, working day and night.

Just as we cannot fully understand the process by which the organic resources in the body of a pregnant woman converge to form an embryo, so it is impossible to comprehend all the processes involved when the reproductive system recoils on itself to produce the embryo of superconsciousness in the brain. The vital energy of the body converges toward this transformation.

The great and rare spiritual geniuses of the past were the products of this biological transformation, either from birth or sometime during their lifetimes. It exists even today in imperfect and abortive forms in the mediums and psychics whose inexplicable performances cause bewilderment among observers.

Both of these manifestations have occurred and continue to occur through the natural products of this metamorphosis—the action of an awakened Kundalini—even though knowledge of the mechanism is entirely absent, or is saturated with ancient superstitions and misconceptions.

What mental prodigies will illumine the world and what colossal changes will be effected when the laws governing this process of transfiguration become known? The outstanding intellects of the world will then undergo effective disciplines to activate the mechanism in themselves to achieve the highest goal possible for humanity.

What I assert might at first sight appear to be impossible—

the wishful dream of a visionary that has no roots in reality. But the science of Kundalini will lead to the fulfillment of the dreams of idealists through the ages, because with this new organ of perception will come the solutions to many of the greatest problems facing us today.

Animal traits and frailties of human beings have been so rampant in history that it can well be considered a delusion to believe that mankind can ever reach a condition of peaceful coexistence, harmony, brotherhood, justice, and plenitude.

Humankind has, however, made progress. We are more aware than people have ever been of the inhumanity among men. This inner process could never be possible unless it had a psychic or biological base or even both. In either case, the brain must have been in some way influenced or molded to allow the trend to be a part of the individual and collective mind.

If this is accepted, then it follows that whatever the nature of the agency, the ideas and behavior of the individuals can retard or accelerate this trend. For the refinement in human behavior and thought there must also occur a corresponding refinement in the brain and nervous system. But since we are entirely unaware of the processes by which the brain functions —and the nature of the energy that is used in its activity—it is idle to expect that we can understand these processes.

This much, however, we know for certain: The religious luminaries of mankind included in their ranks men and women of the loftiest character ever born. High moral caliber goes side by side with an elevated state of consciousness. The psychosomatic instrument to effect this transformation of consciousness and the ennoblement of character is Kundalini. In the ages to come, therefore, the voluntarily created products of Kundalini will not only be mental and intellectual prodigies of the highest order, but also men and women of exemplary character.

There is a weighty reason why this should be so: The entry to the superconscious state implies a thrilling and exhilarating experience; there is nothing of this earth to compare with it.

It is the acme of all that a human being would like to have, possess, or achieve.

"The cow that fulfills all wishes," "the Island of Jewels," "the Garden of Bliss," "the Mountain of Gold," and other such euphemistic terms were coined by the ancient masters to signify the indescribable glory of this sovereign state.

The fears expressed by William Irwin Thompson, that such a crop of adepts would introduce a new papacy and pose a threat to democracy, are unfounded. In the first place, such an attitude presupposes belief in the perpetual nature of the present form of ideas about democracy and other modern political systems, in which cracks have already begun to appear.

Secondly, it completely ignores the actual reality, which allots a dominant position to the intelligent and gifted in a society over their less fortunate compeers. Again, can we reasonably suppose that man can overthrow a system that is rooted in the very base of the universe and human individuality and planned by nature for his evolution; or can we ever succeed in making all men and women equally intelligent and capable, when the very structure of nature exhibits polarities? If such a supposition is unrealistic, as it clearly is, then where is the flaw in what I forecast?

The very nature of the present explosive state of the world makes it imperative that some other class of men than those who now hold the reins of power in the various fields of human activity should occupy their places. They alone can bring harmony where chaos and violence prevail at present.

The present search for "masters," "gurus," "initiators," and "adepts" is a forerunner of the events to come.

I am not worried that intellectuals as a class are apathetic to what I aver. This has always been the situation whenever a new idea was presented to mankind. The intelligentsia forms the most vehement opposition, because the concept is so new and so radically divergent from the thinking of the past that an overhauling of our present-day notions and values is necessary to assimilate it.

What is of paramount importance is that the possibilities

implicit in Kundalini should become known. This is slowly coming to pass, thanks to dedicated efforts of those eager to help in the birth of a new world. This all-out search for a better order and a happier life for humanity will never cease until the objective is won.

II

The Ancient Concept of Kundalini[*]

The idea of Kundalini—the Serpent Power—is not unknown in the West. It finds mention in a veiled way in the Bible, but there are clear mentions of it in the books on alchemy and other esoteric disciplines. In the beginning of this century, an American writer traced references to Kundalini in several passages of the Bible. For some years past, this ancient doctrine has penetrated even into the exclusive precincts of science, and some eminent scientists, at least, have come to know of its implications in the context of the current views about religion and mystical experience.

There is, however, a general attitude of incredulity which is not to be wondered at in the context of the present attitude

* Published as "Understanding Transformation of Consciousness" in *Fields Within Fields*. Issue Number 11, Spring 1974, published by World Institute Council, 777 United Nations Plaza, New York, N.Y. 10017. Publisher: Julius Stulman.

of science toward religion and the supernatural. This attitude has resulted in a curious situation. What we generally see is extreme skepticism on one side and extreme credulity on the other. I am not disturbed by the rather rigid attitude from the ordinary ranks even of science. Considering the climate that has prevailed so far, I welcome it. Too ready a response to a new and unexpected idea is not to be expected of a seasoned intellect. A thorough probe is necessary. What appears to me paradoxical is that some scientists should lend credence to various occurrences, as for instance telekinesis and the possibility of mystical consciousness with the use of drugs, both still debatable propositions, and should hesitate even to accept as a hypothesis that there does exist a dormant source of a still unidentified biological energy which is at the root of all such bizarre or sublime phenomena. Can anyone deny that there must be an explanation in psychosomatic terms for all the transcendental and paranormal phenomena of the human mind? If the phenomena are accepted, then the existence of a causal source for them has also to be admitted. They just cannot occur at random due to causes that must always remain beyond the probe of the intellect. If this position is accepted, then it means that both psychic phenomena and the beatific vision will, to the end of time, continue to puzzle and mystify without any hope of a rational or even suprarational solution of the problem.

As I have said, I am not at all disappointed by the skeptical attitude of the men of science, but what I cannot understand is the inconsistency in their approach to the problem. Without the corroboration of one single great mystic, either of the East or West, many of them have taken it for granted, without a regular investigation, that the conscious, semiconscious or deep-sleep states induced by drugs, biofeedback, autohypnosis or restraint of breathing and blood circulation, represent or are on par with mystical experience, without ever trying to define in the phraseology of science what "mystical experience" means.

There is such a deep gulf of difference between the mystics known to history and the specimens produced by these methods that it does not need any special effort to distinguish between the two. The evidence furnished by all these subjects of investigation—psychic displays, hypnosis, mind-altering drugs, breathing exercises, other forms of Yoga—however trivial they might be, would tend to furnish material to enable men of science to formulate their views about this still uncharted realm. But since we know that, all through the course of history, mystics have been credited with all these states and faculties which scientists are now investigating, namely psychic powers, including telekinesis, clairvoyance, precognition and healing, altered states of consciousness, trance conditions with diminished breathing and pulse, and the like, why shouldn't mystical experience form the taproot of the research and the other occupy a subsidiary place to it?

With a research span extending now to more than ninety years on psi phenomena, have we come any nearer to the understanding of the force responsible for them? Has any psychic healer, spirit raiser, physical medium, clairvoyant, breath-control expert, yogi, etc., been able to specify the force that is working in him? Do they not generally ascribe their extraordinary gifts and performances to a control (like the demon of Socrates), to concentration of mind, to Pranayama, to the favor of a guru, divine grace, and the like? From the avowals made by persons of all these categories, during the past several decades, it is obvious that not one of them has been able to furnish a rational or a convincing explanation for his or her feats or an accurate knowledge of the power working in them. Is not this study—for which we have numerous personal narratives and confessions covering several decades—enough to convince investigating savants that they must look for the explanation somewhere else and not work in a rut in the exploration of a mystery that has baffled all great intellects of the past through the historical period? How can the subjects of these extraordinary phenomena, who are themselves mystified by them, enlighten the men of science who investigate their surprising or weird displays?

A New Dimension of Matter and Consciousness

I am concerned over the issue for several reasons. It is high time now that scientists accept the existence of bio-energy (prana) , the intelligent force behind all chemical actions and reactions of a biological organism. Here we deal with a new dimension of matter and consciousness. The experiments made in Russia and other places to locate bio-energy (apparently the cosmic orgone energy of Reich) are yet in a very rudimentary stage, but as has always happened in the sphere of knowledge, if the idea is based on a solid foundation, the experiments will be successful and the elusive medium will be located one day.

What I suggest is that investigation on Kundalini provides a most practical way to study the action of bio-energy in the transformative processes set afoot in one in whom the Serpent Power is aroused. We have numerous historical instances to show that conversion and transformation of consciousness are possible under certain circumstances. But how does it happen? What are the biological factors responsible for it? We have no means to know at present. The books on Yoga—Indian, Chinese, or Tibetan—ascribe it to the control of mind, breath, and re-productive energy. I have thoroughly verified it upon myself and so have others. Where then lies the difficulty in making this ancient tradition—existing in both the East and West for thousands of years—the subject of study of a few savants to ascertain its validity? How can an open-minded scientist reject a possibility that has been admitted by countless people in the past, including eminent philosophers and mystics, and pass a judgment without moving a finger to ascertain the facts?

My own humble contribution to this ancient tradition (not as a speculative hypothesis but as the direct outcome of my own experience) is that this dormant reservoir of bio-energy is not only responsible for mystical experience and the still baffling psi phenomena, but is also the presently unlocated and still disputed evolutionary mechanism in human beings, as well as the fountainhead of genius and extraordinary talent. What is in this, let us say, supposition to cause reactions of incredulity and skepticism from impartially minded science? The only reason is that the idea is so remote from the current thinking of an average scientist as to be unacceptable. Coming from a scientist, it would have value. But that does not mean that what I am asserting, without being a scientist, cannot have the germs of a still unsuspected scientific discovery in it.

Let us take as an example the studies of the phenomenon of sleep. Only two decades earlier some of the dramatic disclosures now made were not only unknown but may not even have been believed. Even with all the research done so far, the mystery of the REM phase, peculiar to mammals, stands unsolved. There must be some very solid reason behind it. We still stand at the fringe of the mystery of life, and nothing can be more prejudicial to the study of mind and consciousness than a closed-door attitude toward new ideas and views that may not appear strictly scientific for a moment, or that may not be clothed in the language of science. It has been observed that deprivation of REM sleep for a period of several days in succession has a tremendous effect not only on people but even on animals. They become abnormal and behave in strange ways. There occurs loss of attention and avoidance of work in human beings. A man of steady character may become irresponsible and flippant, behaving in a manner as he would never do in a normal state. Why I am very much concerned over the issue is that just as deprivation of REM sleep creates certain abnormal conditions of mind, in the same way deprivation of a healthy environment, at an advanced stage of human evolution, creates abnormal tendencies in the human mind, impossible to remedy unless the environment is changed.

What Underlies Present Social Upheaval?

Kundalini is the guardian of human evolution. Traditionally she is known as Durga the creatrix, Chandi the fierce and bloodthirsty, and Kali the destroyer. She is also Bhajangi the serpent. As Chandi or Kali she has a garland of skulls around her neck and drinks human blood. What can be behind this hideous picture of a divine being? What led the ancient masters to depict such a ghastly likeness of the goddess? It is true that conceived as both the creatrix and the destroyer, in the cosmo- logical sense, she could only be portrayed with a frightful aspect for the latter role. But then why a serpent which stings and why Chandi the fierce? There is a profound significance not only in these awful portraits of the Shakti (divine energy) but also in many other rituals and ceremonies of Tantric worship as also modes of initiations to the cult. The power, when aroused in a body not attuned to it with the help of various disciplines or not genetically mature for it, can lead to awful mental states, to almost every form of mental disorder, from hardly noticeable aberrations to the most horrible forms of insanity, to neurotic and paranoid states, to megalomania and, by causing tormenting pressure on reproductive organs, to an all-consuming sexual thirst that is never assuaged (see Chapter 6). I am not telling a fairy tale conjured up by my imagination but have experienced the hard realities of this yet little-known phenomenon not only on myself but met it in the case of scores of other people both in India and abroad, and treated some of them back to sanity and health. Let a team of open-minded scientists, in the service of knowledge, call by means of wide publicity for personal histories of people who have had or are having Kundalini experiences in Europe, America, and the East, and the result, I am sure, will be a flood of letters from people in all spheres and walks of life. Many of these will, no doubt, be fictitious from hysterics and cranks, but there would still remain a large percentage of genuine cases which, on in- vestigation, can provide incontestable evidence of what I say.

The fact that Hatha Yoga practices can lead to insanity is widely known in India and, to some extent, even in the West. The term "mastana" in Persian and "avadhoot" in Sanskrit is applied to an initiate whose entry to higher dimensions of consciousness is attended with loss of worldly sense to an extent as to be oblivious of his behavior or, in other words, who while attaining to higher perception loses control over himself. Cases of this category can be met in India and, probably, in other places also. All this association of Kundalini and its products with possible derangement of mind, during the course of practice and even later, can definitely mean, even if we disbelieve other things, that the practices of Hatha Yoga or the arousal of the Serpent Power can have such a drastic effect on the body and the brain as to cause unhingement of reason in some practitioners. Apart from every other consideration, does not even this issue provide a strong incentive for an earnest scientist to start an investigation on this type of Yoga? If the practices or the alleged arousal of the power can, in some cases, lead to psychosis, looked at from the other angle, can it not be possible that the spontaneous arousal of the power, brought about by genetic factors in an unadjusted system, is a fertile cause for many forms of insanity and other mental or nervous disorders?

The Bliss of Ananda

"Flawless, exceedingly sweet and beautiful, soul enchanting, uninterrupted flow of words (in speech or writing) manifests itself on all sides in them (devotees blessed with genius) who keep you, O Shakti (energy) of Shiva (universal consciousness), the destroyer of Kamadeva (Cupid), constantly in their mind," says *Panchastavi,* a highly esoteric work on Kundalini (3.12). "They see you shining with the stainless, pale luster of the moon in the head, seated on a gleaming lotus throne, sparkling with the white glitter of snow, sprinkling nectar on the petals of the lotuses both in the muladhara (the root-center close to the organ of generation) and Brahma-Randra (the cavity of Brahma in the head corresponding to the ventricular cavity)."

In spite of my knowledge of the fact that any allusion to any ancient work on a religious subject is anathema to some scholars who think, like the intellectuals of sundry vanished civilizations of the past, that they have reached the end of knowledge, I have purposely reproduced this verse from a work more than a thousand years old to show that what I am stating has confirmative evidence of the past. The verse mentions the gift of genius and, what is as important, the flow of the gleaming radiation and the potent generative fluids from the muladhara chakra, i.e., the reproductive region, to the brain through the spinal cord. The language is metaphoric, but the allusions are clear beyond the least shadow of doubt. The sparkling radiation is white like snow. Sometimes it is likened to camphor and sometimes to milk. The ambrosia is the nectarlike reproductive secretion which, at the highest point of ecstasy, pours into the brain with such an intensely pleasurable sensation that even the sexual orgasm pales into insignificance before it. This unbelievably rapturous sensation—pervading the whole of the spinal cord, the organs of generation and the brain—is nature's incentive to the effort directed at self-transcendence, as the orgasm is the incentive for the reproductive act. In the later stages the sensation ceases and a perennially blissful consciousness becomes a permanent or occasional feature of the successful initiate's life.

The bliss of ananda, repeatedly mentioned in the manuals on Yoga and other spiritual lore of India, refers to the transformed rapturous consciousness created by the flow of the bio-energy drawn from the nerves feeding the reproductive system and spread all over the human frame. They are the nadis of the Hatha Yoga and Raja Yoga manuals. The distinguishing feature between this bio-energy and that normally feeding the brain is that the former appears like a glowing radiance in the head, spread around the body and, when the attention is directed inward, spreading far and wide to reveal a throbbing world of lustrous, intensely blissful life. The single-pointed attention of the talented writer, poet, musician, scientist, and painter or thinker and the moods of intense absorption experienced during creative periods, attended by a sense of satisfaction and even joy, felt by every creative mind at its handiwork, both depend on the operation of Kundalini. The gifted child who neglects his play or other form of amusement and sits absorbed in some book or an experiment or a work of art, is blessed with an emanation from the same source. In mystical experience, beatific state, transcendence or Samadhi, the same bio-energy rushing up in a much more powerful stream creates the transports of inexpressible bliss and the intensely absorbed state of ecstasy.

Kundalini: The Biological Lever

The peace and bliss, and also enhancement in their creative ability, experienced by some of those practicing healthy forms of Yoga, owe their origin to Kundalini. The mental and physical well-being, and also the cure of sundry ailments sometimes effected, are often due to its regenerative office. There is no sphere of human activity and thought in which the impact of the evolutionary apparatus is not felt. Once the mechanism is recognized there would be no scientific study as extensive and as fraught with momentous consequences for mankind as this. This is the fountainhead of all that is productive, noble, heroic, and sublime in man. The human body, with its extremely complex formation and with still many unexplored functions and processes, particularly those occurring in the brain and nervous system, is yet an enigma to science.

The modern, more elaborate, methods of research are bringing new facts and new data to light that were not even suspected before. There are many eminent scientists, engaged in the study of Yoga, who stand amazed and, sometimes, even incredulous before the mastery over the subconscious and the metabolic rhythms of the body displayed by some yogis who have gained control over their autonomic nervous system. This possibility has been known and made use of in India for thousands of years but is a surprising experience for modern science. In the same way the psychosomatic mechanism of Kundalini, the biological lever in every form of Yoga, with its implications and possibilities, has been known and made use of in India constantly for thousands of years, from the time of the Indus Valley civilization. This culture, as fresh investigation has shown, had a lively intercourse in trade and culture with America of that day, and was the possible initiator in the cultivation of cotton on the Peruvian coast, more than two thousand years before the birth of Christ, centuries before the cultivation was undertaken in Egypt. I have mentioned this to show that references to Kundalini in the Maya scripture of the Zunis, called the Popul Vuh, where it is named "Hura-Kan," or lightning, must also have an Indian origin. In Egypt the minute snake on the headdress of the pharaohs carried the same significance.

There are unmistakable references to Kundalini in the Bible. The circumstances attending the birth of Christ have some features common with those attending the birth of Krishna, the lord of yogis who in his childhood dances on the head of the venomous snake, Kali-Naga, that is the Serpent Power. To me it seems ironic that a cult so ancient, so widespread as to be global, and so well supported by the evidence of some of the loftiest intellects of the world, including Plato, Shankaracharya, Lao-Tse and others, should be a closed book to the intelligentsia of our time. Like the body control demonstrations of yogis that also were a closed book to science, investigation into Kundalini is likely to prove an even more stunning experience for scientists who undertake this research in the exciting days to come.

Do not the physical phenomena, exhibited under test conditions, by some individuals gifted with psi faculties present an enigma that is inexplicable for science? And are not scientists themselves divided on the issue of psi phenomena, and even the phenomenon of life itself? Thus while for Jacques Monod the existence of man is the result of an accident, for Sir Alister Hardy, another eminent biologist, psychical research suggests that a dualistic view of man is highly possible, and that there is enough empirical evidence to support belief in a "divine flame," pervading the universe, accessible to the seeking human mind. In spite of the performances of physical mediums like Eusapia Palladino, Daniel Douglas Home, Rudi Schneider and other gifted individuals like Edgar Cayce, and the testimony of eminent scholars and men of science like William James, Henri Bergson, C. D. Broad, William McDougall, Sir Oliver Lodge, and even Carl Jung, the attitude of academicians toward mind and consciousness of the phenomena associated with religion and the supernatural is still on the whole apathetic. The research now being done in Russia, and on Uri Geller and others in America and Europe, and on yogis in India, and on psychic healers in other parts of the world who allegedly use common knives or their bare hands for major operations, is not likely to prove any more decisive in settling the issue for the simple reason that the mysterious force behind all these remarkable phenomena is not amenable to human control and therefore will always remain unidentified by any means adopted by science.

But this apathetic attitude toward the issues of faith of scientists in general and the division among the ranks of scholars over the validity of psychic phenomena is fraught with the gravest consequences for the masses, who have neither time nor the mental acumen to reach to the bottom of the problem or to sift the genuine from the false. The irresistible pressure of evolutionary processes creates a burning thirst for self-knowledge, the natural prelude for entry to another dimension of consciousness. When those tormented by this thirst encounter a blank if they turn to scholars for guidance, and at best an indigestible dose of polemics, what other alternative remains for them except to fall back on those who profess knowledge of this sublime subject, whoever they be? Their mutiny springs from the defeat in their bid to know the meaning of life. How do modern psychologists account for this revolt which is still gaining momentum? Hysteria, repression, regression, wish-fulfillment, uncontrollable unconscious impulses, or what? Into which of their pet categories do they classify this almost universal mental wave of disillusionment with the established values and orders and the gnawing hunger for a more satisfying spiritually oriented life? Is it the unconscious threat to their survival, posed by the nuclear arsenals of the world, which is at the bottom of their inexplicable mental behavior?

Recently in Srinagar I had visits from an intelligent young man, the only son of an affluent American, who said that he preferred a calm life of meditation and self-searching in comparison to luxury and abundant wealth. There are millions of young men and women who think the same way. Do you not see in this rebellion the same which happened in India millennia ago when Buddha left his kingdom for the forest? The growing impact of evolutionary forces creates a sensitiveness which refuses to remain subservient to a mechanistic way of life. Do you know how the wise men in ancient India met practically the same mental situation after a few hundred years of affluent civilized life? They divided the span of human life into four parts, assigning the last two, beginning from about the age of fifty, for the quest of the self. During the third period they made their abode in a forest, even accompanied by their wives, supported by their children, engaged in meditation and other spiritual exercises, absolved from the other duties of life.

Taking a Planetary Point of View

You have to look at the issue of human evolution from an aeonian and a planetary point of view, embracing the whole civilized history of mankind and not only from the still extremely narrow outlook of science. Man cannot forever live happily on skyscrapers, cars, airplanes, ships, television sets, radios, computers, and other productions of technology, nor will he continue for long to feel thrilled with the exciting accounts of astronomers and space explorers, as is the case today. There must come a point of satiation with repeated doses of the same stuff, if his principal question is not answered, and this question orbits around his own self. We already see the signs of this satiety. If scientists do not move out of their present narrow orbit and stop harping on the same old refrain, the day is not distant when the more dogmatic of them will not carry any weight in a rebellious society. This has started to happen even now. The consequences of this are catastrophic for legions. Are any of the millions who take to drugs and vagrant ways of life prepared to listen to reason or to the analysis of a psychologist? What ancient Indian adepts clearly understood and prudently provided for, the modern leaders of thought, because of a warped mental outlook, failed to grasp and safeguard in time. The result is that the lives of thousands of raw teenagers, who could hardly decide for themselves, have been drawn into a vortex from which it is difficult to rescue them. A cheat who defrauds a person of one single dollar is a criminal in the eyes of the law, but what about the impostor who draws innocent lives, unable to judge for themselves, into the meshes of a loose, indolent, orgiastic, and unfruitful life by a false pretense of spiritual knowledge.

There are hundreds of thousands of bright young men and women suffering unbearable torment and enduring debasing poverty for their mistaken ideas. But with the intellectual world completely divided over this issue, how can they be helped? Irrational trends in thinking and unrealistic beliefs that could not have found acceptance from intelligent sections of society, even during medieval times, are cherished with religious reverence by crowds, ready to pin their faith on anything that can draw them out of the irrationally "rational" scientific and mechanistic thinking of the empiricist hierarchy of our time. In face of the mounting evidence to show that other interpretations for the cosmos and other explanations for life and consciousness are possible, the monotonous drone of even eminent men of science of the old ideas and views is almost sickening, and it is no wonder that a stampede has started against such a rationalism. The unbelievably fantastic accounts of Brazilian sorcerers, Indian yogis, and Tibetan adepts, some of which have become instant best sellers, carrying the readers into unrealistic worlds of fantasy, magic, and myth, unmistakably point to a change in the attitude of the reading public. They avidly seek for corroboration of their own growing antimechanistic and antirational tendencies of the mind. They like to listen to fairy tales and to stories from modern Arabian Nights to draw themselves out of the relentless cycle of rational thought in a universe where they are sternly made to believe that they are no more than tiny cogs in a gigantic social machine, no more than individual members of a colony of ants.

The Brazilian sorcerers, Indian master-yogis, and Tibetan adepts, capable of incredible feats, never appear on the scene in person. No one sees them face to face or has even their correct address. Nor are the stories verified nor is verification demanded. Whether imaginary or real, they serve their purpose to entertain the hungry mind for a while and that is enough. This much is sure: They will never be seen and never verified.

But that does not matter. As one of the admirers of Carlos Castaneda puts it: If the account is a documentary truth, then Castaneda is a great anthropologist; if it is an imaginative tale, then he is a master fiction writer. In either case he wins. How can we reply to this argument? Another and an even more fantastic story or adventure may be around the corner, starting a new sensation and a fresh hunt. How can you cure the hunger for these fantastic tales of the occult and the supernatural, these mental peregrinations into the world of the miracle-working yogi, sorcerer, and the magician? It has persisted through history. The primitive myths, on which a totally different interpretation has been put by Freudian psychologists, owe their origin to the same impulse in the human mind. The sudden upsurge of this hunger for the irrational and the bizarre in a strictly rational age, in contravention of the canons of the established order, lends a new dimension to this impulse which it could never attain in the context of a primitive society. But what is the reason for this mysterious urge, this search for the preternatural, eerie, and fabulous by the human psyche? Where will it land the seekers of today?

A Driving Impulse to Understand

A new orientation and a new study is necessary for science if a catastrophe is to be averted. A whole universe of unbelievable wonders exists in the consciousness of man. Every incentive to listen to the mythical, the fantastic, and the fabulous comes from within. Every impulse to explore the weird, the supernatural, and the bizarre rises out of the unfathomed depths of consciousness. Those scientists and scholars who devote themselves to this study have the impulse more strongly marked than the others. They persist in the investigation sometimes even against the incredulous smiles and even gibes of their incorrigibly skeptical colleagues in whom the impulse, for various causes which will be discussed in detail elsewhere, is wholly or partially absent. A frigid woman looks with disdain at the passionate nature of a friend and often considers herself

superior to her, oblivious to the lack. A stunted impulse at self-transcendence and lack of curiosity for the mystical and tran-
the individual and the race. Therefore, those who, like the
the individual and the race. Therefore, those who, like the
frigid woman, pride themselves on their inflexible down-to-earth attitude, in spite of convincing testimony to the contrary, disclose a lack of sufficient interest in the "numinous," an indispensable prerequisite for mystical experience and the beatific trance. They do not realize their own shortcomings, like Bertrand Russell who, when confronted with the weighty evidence provided by psychical research for survival in some form, observed that although the psychical evidence was strong enough, the biological evidence against survival was even stronger. What biological evidence? Had we reached the rock-bottom of biology in his time or have we reached it even now? Are not new ultramicroscopic levels and new, then-unthought-of life-energies slowly shaping themselves out with the present-day more sophisticated methods and instruments of research? What then lies behind this negative attitude when the investigation has not reached a decisive stage? The present insurgence arises from death-blows of this nature aimed at the aspirations of man. Since a transcendental state of consciousness is the evolutionary target for mankind, lack of interest in the "numinous" and the "divine" denotes a sterility for which no amount of "intellectualism" can compensate.

Skepticism, apathy, and coldness toward this issue from leading scientists and scholars is dangerous because, denied the appropriate guidance or answer, the eagerly searching crowds will go to the other extreme, as they have already started doing, and prefer extreme credulity to excessive positivism. A look at the psychic and occult books, magazines, brochures, and papers, published the world over, should leave no one in doubt that, despite the reticence of the leaders of thought, the masses are clubbing together into countless societies, sects, brotherhoods, and groups for adventurous sorties into the occult. Who is to prevent them? Now sundry scientists and scholars, carried away by their enthusiasm, are joining their ranks. They even wear saffron robes and outlandish dresses aggressively to proclaim their participation. If the present position continues, in a decade or two there may occur a stampede in the ranks of scientists too, not only in the capitalist but in the communist states also, for the pressure of the evolutionary forces is irresistible. One of the proofs for what I say will lie in this growing ferment in the individual pools of consciousness throughout the world, slowly building itself up in a storm, unless a fresh, spiritually oriented social order and way of thinking come into existence before it bursts and damage is done.

What I assert may seem imaginary and fantastic to the ultra-conservatives, but it is not as fantastic as the reality. Denial of Divinity involves a denial of the most exciting adventure and the most exquisite and thrilling mental feast possible for man. The magnetic field that draws the needle of the mind to turn always toward happiness is the soul itself. The inexhaustible mine of marvels, of superhuman powers, paranormal gifts, magical prowess, supernatural visions, uncanny sights, and miraculous feats is consciousness alone. Whatever the approach to the supernatural, the occult, and the divine, the ultimate target will remain the same, for the soul will never rest content until it has the beatific vision of itself. Those who take to Yoga or any other occult practice or spiritual discipline, even if they gain a certain amount of calm or a deeper insight than before, will still continue to try other methods and disciplines until the Supreme Light is experienced. Then alone the search of the intellect comes to rest. "That in which the mind finds rest, quieted by the practice of yoga, that in which a man, seeing the Self by the Self in the Self is satisfied," says the Bhagavad Gita (6.20 and 21), "that in which he findeth the Supreme Delight which reason can grasp beyond the senses, wherein established he moveth not from the reality . . . that should be known by the name of yoga, this disconnection from the union with pain. This yoga must be clung to with a firm conviction and with undesponding mind."

The Lesson of the Musk Deer

The Indian adepts liken the exteriorized restless seeking of the mind, running in this direction or that to encounter the supernatural and the numinous, to the antics of a musk deer which, uncomprehending of the fact that the fragrance emanates from its own navel, gallops here and there in search of it. Whatever turn the present rush for Yoga, Zen, Sufism, drugs, mantras, occult powers, psychic gifts, spiritualism, or psi phenomena takes and whatever hunt for yogis, masters, adepts, magicians, and sorcerers ensues, the final outcome of all this fret and fever, I am sure, will turn out the same—to wit, the development of scientifically oriented methods of self-knowledge, the ultimate target of every spiritual quest undertaken by any known illuminated saint or seer of the past. I can safely predict that younger ranks of scientists will see this revolution coming to pass. Why I am sanguine about this is that the phenomenon we are witnessing in many parts of the earth must be based on a common cause, must have a common factor underlying it in the psychosomatic organism of man. It cannot be a random affair, for it has repeated historical precedents, and even today there are nearly six million mendicant ascetics (Saddhus) roaming in different parts of India on exactly the same quest. The psychosomatic cause is Kundalini. The hunger for the supernatural and the divine or for inner exploration arises due to its pressure on the brain, as the hunger for carnal knowledge springs from its pressure on the reproductive base. Only I fervently wish that, because of further apathy or vacillation on the part of the intellectual community, it may not cause further ruination of lives, blasting of careers, and disruption of families, as it is doing now.

The traditional concept expressed in the verse from *Panchastavi*, already reproduced, refers to Shiva or universal consciousness as the destroyer of Kamadeva, i.e., Cupid. This has a deep significance. In a healthy and harmonized system, on the arousal of Kundalini, a constant stream of sublimated reproductive energy, in radiating waves, rises into the brain, causing an in-

expressible state of rapture and a breathtaking, marvelous transformation of consciousness. The pressure on the organs of generation is instantly released and the sexual appetite diminished
or completely lost. This is the reason many mystics led a monastic or celibate life and evinced an antipathy toward marriage
or even toward free intercourse with members of the opposite
sex. There have also been mystics and yogis who passed a
married life and had children even after enlightenment. Most
seers of the Upanishads and most of the Vedic sages were married men and women. There are clear references in the works
of the well-known philosophers Abhinava Gupta and Shankaracharya to Urdhava Retas, i.e., the capacity gained by accomplished yogis to carry the reproductive essences into the
Brahma-Randra in the brain. The books on Hatha Yoga and
the Tantras often allude to this state. The Chinese and Tibetan
treatises on Yoga and meditation also contain detailed description of and methods for attaining this condition.

The question is: Are all these statements and assertions mere
flights of fancy or is there a solid foundation behind them? In
India alone there is incontrovertible evidence to show that
belief in and practice of this cult has persisted for no less than
five thousand years. The evidence from Tibet, China, and
Japan, also extending for thousands of years, makes the position
almost unassailable. The system of Hara in Japan also believes
in the existence of a power-reservoir below the navel. Can we
reject all this testimony as idiocy, superstition, or delusion?
If not, what have we done to study this phenomenon? The first
and last aim of Yoga, according to every ancient authoritative
book on the subject, is to stimulate the chakras (nerve-concen-
trations) of the cerebrospinal system to activate Kundalini. It
is tragic that some very open-minded and learned scientists, at
the moment engaged in the study of Yoga, show a lack of
awareness of this fact. Both Shivananda and Vivekananda, two
of the foremost exponents of Yoga in recent times, make allusions in their books on Yoga to "ojas," or sublimated sex energy
that feeds the brain in transcendental states of consciousness.
In the practice of meditation all great masters stress the urgent

need for avoiding sleepiness, drowziness, wandering of thoughts, daydreaming, emptiness, haziness, or semiawake states to enable the effort to have the right impact on the brain. It has always been known in India that the relaxation of grip on the mind during meditation can lead to autohypnosis and even other undesirable psychic conditions. The yogi must learn to concentrate on the divine or on the image of God or other deity or even a center in the body—as, for instance, the navel or the heart, or a mantra—more intensely than a mathematician or a scientist concentrates on a problem. I shall elaborate this issue in another work, supported with authorities from the past. Here it is sufficient to point out that whatever the method of meditation, the somatic chord that is touched and made to vibrate is Kundalini. This is the reason for the eroticism connected with mysticism of both the East and West.

To Explain the Inexplicable

The first thing that should strike a keenly observant man of science, when he comes across certain phenomena connected with Yoga, is whether the feats cannot be duplicated in any other way, as for instance with hypnosis or autosuggestion. If a hypnoid explanation is not feasible, as for instance in perennial waking ecstasy the state ascribed to Ramana Maharshi and many other saints), in clairvoyance, prescience, and other paranormal faculties, then the point that should arise is how, in a strictly conditioned organism, which has been constantly under the observation of scientists for the past hundreds of years, both in its normal and abnormal functioning, there occur possibilities in certain gifted individuals that are entirely inexplicable in terms of the known categories of scientific knowledge. They cannot be a random affair, beyond the reach of a rational explanation, for they show a basic similarity and rhythm that cannot be ascribed to purely chance occurrences. Would it not help investigation if, instead of groping in the dark and attempting irrational explanations, as is sometimes being done now, we assume a biological possibility in the human body which has not been studied or even suspected so far? Acting on this possibility, the first concern of those engaged in this research should be to make a thorough study of the ancient documents dealing with Yoga, mystical experience, magic, occultism, and alchemy, particularly those that advocate the existence of hidden powers in man, and then design the empirical investigation in the light of the knowledge gained by this study.

It would be idle to expect an instantaneous or magical outcome of this investigation. Such an attitude of mind would be highly unscientific. No enlightened individual, through the whole course of history, was able to furnish a rational and comprehensive explanation for the extraordinary state of his mind. If any scholar or any group of scientists is of the view that any spiritual teacher can clear this position overnight, that individual or group would never see the dream realized. The same effort and dedication that led to the discovery of the physical laws of nature are necessary for unraveling the mysteries of the spirit also. It may be that the effort and dedication needed for the latter would be even greater, for this is the primordial quest of man. All other investigations and all the resources developed by science are auxiliary as compared to it. I know it will be a colossal investigation that will, perhaps, never come to an end, for it will cover not only religious experience and psi phenomena, but insanity, neurosis, genius, and other abnormal or extraordinary manifestations of the human mind. Even after scores of years of ceaseless experimentation, the existing riddles facing science still stand unsolved. When this is the position with regard to common problems and events that are either always present before us or recur continually, what should be the state of investigation of a mysterious phenomenon that is not only rare or elusive but also has, at the moment, no visible physical base to which we can hold. I am the last person to wish to be known as a miracle worker or an adept. I am only a humble human being, with many frailties and failings who—call it chance or divine providence—stumbled on a secret which I wish to share with other fellow beings. I have no pretension to learning or high distinction in any branch of art or science.

Coming from a distinguished scientist or scholar, and couched in the language of science or with a sprinkling of erudition, the same idea might have met with instant response or even acceptance, not on its own merits but because of its association with a high-sounding name or with the familiar pattern of the language used. Wanting in both, this disclosure, which I predict will form the most highly honored and important study of our progeny, is still shrouded in oblivion because it has no eminent authority to bruit it aloud.

The question that can reasonably be asked of me is what empirical evidence I can produce in support of my avowals. Can the existence of the psychosomatic powerhouse of Kundalini be demonstrated to the satisfaction of an empiricist? My answer to this repeatedly asked question is positively in the affirmative. It can be readily inferred that if I had any doubts about it I would not come with positive statements but would try to evade or prevaricate. Why should I involve myself at all in a controversy with scholars and men of science and not go straight to the crowd with a fascinating story or even many stories, for which there is more than enough material in my experiences in the plane of higher consciousness and also in the sphere of my activities in the social and, indirectly, political fields. With very little expenditure of energy, I could put half a dozen exciting volumes on the market, supported with unimpeachable evidence, to show that I am not romancing. I know very well that no questions would be asked and, in the climate now prevailing in Europe and America, I could even draw upon my imagination to make the stories even more thrilling and breathtaking to absorb the readers. I know I could gain both name, wealth, and popularity and would be much more sought after than I am now. I could do this but I will not because of my rigid adherence to my resolve—a spontaneous impulse born of my rare experience—to make this mighty secret of nature known to the world in a way that it is accepted as a universal truth, with empirical support, and becomes the common property of all mankind, free of personality factors, schisms, and sectarianism, like all other discoveries and achievements of science.

The chief motivating factor for this frame of mind is the present desperate situation of the world. The entry into the higher dimensions of consciousness gives to the mind an acuity of perception into the future. What it discloses is a picture so awful that I wish with all my heart that by some act of grace mankind might be saved the horror of it. The world stands in dire need of a speedy breakthrough in the science of the spirit, and the phenomenon of Kundalini, when verified, seems to me to be the only answer to the present disruption and dilemma. The disclosure, when empirically established, would save millions from wreck and ruination, from deceit, fraud, and exploitation, and benefit countless millions more in deciding upon a safe and healthy way to assuage their burning thirst for the occult and the divine.

If Freud Had Glimpsed the Transcendental . . .

One single distinguished psychologist or biologist or even a great physician or surgeon, blessed with the same experience that I have or that fell to the share of the great mystics of the past, could prove instrumental in causing a revolution in thought, as Freud did. Freud, however, showed excessive, even mistaken, emphasis only on one aspect of the life-energy which he called libido. This sexualized élan vital is, in terms of Freudian psychology, the archstone of human life. It is the foundation of man's character, the bedrock of his mental traits, the guardian of his family life, the fountainhead of poetry, drama, romance, chivalry and his life, the bestower of genius, the mainspring of his love, loyalty, attachment, and devotion, the architect of civilization and, at the same time, the demon of his envy, jealousy, hate, and aggression. When repressed, disoriented or frustrated, especially in childhood, it may take the monstrous form of mental aberration, perversion, neurosis, and insanity. Perhaps no other psychologist had such a tremendous influence on the thinking of mankind as Sigmund Freud. Do I not represent Kundalini in the same terms without the extremism of Freud? Is not Kundalini also the sexual life current? I even define its somatic character. Where lies the difference then between what I say and what is generally accepted by all Freudian psychologists of today? The main point of difference between us is this: That the ubiquitous libido of Freud is not merely the eros, but much more, namely the central fount of life-energy which acts both for propagation and evolution. The moment this is accepted, the angularities and extremes of the Freudian hypothesis disappear. The frantic, even morbid, efforts made to interpret everything in terms of sex can be plainly traced to an error. While the multisided effect of the powerful sex impulse can be clearly noticed in many spheres of human thought and act, it is plain that other influences also come into play, as for instance, urge to power and wealth, desire for name and fame, thirst for self-knowledge, the lure of the supernatural and the occult, and the like, which has profoundly shaped the life of man.

Since mystical experience and the concepts of religion did not dovetail with his hypothesis, Freud quietly set upon the task to uproot the whole edifice of religion and the supernatural. They were nothing more than pathological states of the mind, a regression of childhood narcissism that sets store on an illusion to gratify itself. These formulations, one can plainly see, have had a pernicious effect on the thinking of a large percentage of modern psychologists. For many of them it is even difficult now to extricate themselves from the chains forged at an early age to bind their mind firmly in disbelief and doubt. Had Freud, like Dr. R. M. Bucke, even one glimpse of the transcendental, his whole pattern of thought might have changed and his prodigious influence caused a healthy revival of spiritual science. The day is not distant when the transpersonal trends in psychology and psychiatry, already started, will completely sweep away the sacrilegious area of his speculation. There is no answer in any system of modern psychology to the challenge posed by the revolt of the rising generations and the entirely unexpected trends of thought met in them. Why this upheaval has occurred is not difficult to understand. We all

know what happened whenever a political system became des-
potic and oppressive, a social system exacting and corrupt, and
a religious system excessively authoritarian and dogmatic.
There arose a demand for revision and reform. Political revolu-
tionaries, reformers, and prophets appeared on the scene. The
old system was overthrown, often with dreadful bloodshed,
suffering, and pain and a new one installed in its place. The
same may happen to the present overbearing and dogmatic
trends in knowledge. There may be a revolution, which has
already started, and it may not stop until radical changes are
effected. "The attempt to combine wisdom and power," said
Albert Einstein, "has only rarely been successful, and then only
for a short while."

Even a child can see that any attempt to interpret all abnormal or paranormal manifestations of the human mind purely
in terms of the psyche is an entirely unscientific way of explain-
ing the phenomena. The channel of expression of mind is the
brain. Whatever the nature of the mind expressed, from the
smallest organism to man, there is invariably a biological organ
to express it. When we take it for granted that a normal human
mind functions through a certain organic structure of the
brain, what makes us suppose that its abnormal or paranormal
expressions can occur without causing appreciable changes in
it? True, changes were not and are not, even now, clearly discernible, but that should be an incentive for devising more
sensitive instruments and more effective methods of investigation and not, like Freud, for taking speculation to fantastic
lengths to account for the phenomena. What Freud did in his
day some scientists and psychologists are even now doing with
regard to the inexplicable phenomena connected with religion
and the occult. The neurotic and the psychotic, with all their
changing moods, eccentricity, erratic behavior, fear, anxiety,
hate, violence, aggression, awfully depressive or excited phases,
persecutions, delusions, obsessions, and fixations have, like a
normal man, a personality of their own. A personality, alien-
ated and distorted no doubt, but a personality nevertheless.
Each case of mental disorder has a well-marked character of its

own and, apart from the appearance of the body, can be clearly recognized by his or her peculiar mental traits, as we can recognize normal men and women by theirs. This definitely points to a basically altered neuronic structure or composition and also to alterations in the bio-energy supplying the brain.

I am positive about this because I have myself come across some cases in which neurosis and insanity appeared soon after the awakening of Kundalini. I am also in touch with cases in which the arousal has led to frightening or mind-shattering experiences. The libido, to use the name adopted by Freud, must have roots deep in the biochemical structure of the body. The fact that it can affect human behavior in drastic ways, and even violently change the whole pattern of life, is clear testimony to its influence on the chemistry of the body. Its expression through the evolutionary channel, i.e., the brain, is subject to the influence of countless factors connected with the life, environment, and the family history of an individual. When even slightly tainted or stained, due to various causes such as a wrong mode of life, unhealthy environment, faulty heredity, shock, frustration, repression, tension, and numerous other factors, it becomes the direct cause of mental and nervous derangement. The ignorance of scientists about the nature and composition of bio-energy is at the root of the schisms and the confusion prevailing in the realm of psychology. It is incredible how any psychologist, with a somatic bias in his beliefs, can disassociate consciousness from the condition of the brain. If the mind is abnormal, the brain too must be a shareholder in the abnormality expressed. According to the latest research, there is a confirmation of the position that the horrifying visions and auditions of the insane have their root—in certain kinds of disorder—in subtle changes in some neuronic structures in the cranium. The real root is an impure or toxic condition of the bio-energy. The susceptibility to mental distemper, noticed in the men of genius, and the extreme care enjoined on yogis in every detail of life in the ancient scriptural lore of India, arise from this reason. When pure, the bio-energy released by Kundalini causes the transports of ecstasy and the flow of genius, and when toxic, the nightmares of insanity.

Adopting Bio-energy as a Working Hypothesis

It amuses me when I see scientists, justifiably proud of their knowledge, summarily dismiss what I say as unrealistic, even preposterous. What is a mystery to me is this: On what grounds do they base their instant judgment? Does what I say violate any biological principle or law? In the present stage of our knowledge of the brain and the nervous system, is it abhorrent for a man of science to assume the existence of a living energy responsible for the phenomenon of life? If not, where lies the harm in accepting what I say as a working hypothesis for an empirical verification? The idea, I agree, is entirely novel and is broached for the first time. But that is no reason to assume beforehand that it cannot be true. If a new idea that has a certain amount of plausibility is viewed with suspicion and mistrust from the very start by men of learning, then how can knowledge grow? "I know nothing except the fact of my ignorance," said Socrates, in spite of his prodigious knowledge compared to the standards of his day. Time has proved him correct to this extent, that we now know much more. How can we know that something similar to what I affirm would not disprove, in the years to come, many of the learned views about the mind and consciousness voiced proudly by the savants today?

It is possible your concept of Yoga might be wrong. From time immemorial, in the country of its birth, Yoga has been universally accepted as a path to self-discipline, with the avowed object of gaining approach to the reality behind the phenomenal world. The names of the accomplished products of Yoga are household words in India. The discipline is primarily oriented to a relatively calm, pastoral society. Some of the modern exponents have reduced it to the position of a sedative or sleeping tablet, of which a daily dose is necessary to reduce tension and bring deep sleep in a highly complex and competitive environment. The calming and soporific properties of Yoga are not an answer to the real question that is agitating the youth of today. When the first excitement is over, the state of disillusionment and dissatisfaction will again supervene. With the methods now in use have we produced even one Walt Whitman, Eckhart, Swedenborg, or Aurobindo, although millions are now practicing Yoga? Sedatives and sleeping pills—necessary to combat the vicious effect on the nerves in a tense, unnatural environment—cannot open the windows of the soul. To assume that the alpha state, a sleepy condition, or hypnosis is enlightenment is incorrect. Such an assumption is fraught with grave consequences. An enlightened consciousness is never possible without a biological transformation. That is the reason the phenomenon has been so rare in history. Whenever it occurred, a great mind invariably emerged.

In a harmonious environment and in a healthy disciplined system, Yoga provides the channel for the cultivation of genius and paranormal faculties of the mind. When more knowledge about this highly complex and mysterious power-mechanism is gained, there will be no limit to the benefits, mental and physical, that can be derived from it. How the transformation of the genes is effected through a rejuvenative activity of the reproductive system, on the arousal of the Serpent Power, and how the seminal fluid in men is sent in a cascading stream of radiant energy to the brain and other vital organs—kept closely guarded secrets by the adepts of the past—forms a breathaking story of the still hidden secrets of nature and will be narrated in its proper time. The same happens with the female hormones and secretions. The rejuvenative and transformative process set afoot is a marvelous phenomenon that has no parallel anywhere.

Guidelines for Clinical Investigation

How can it be possible that such a well-marked, extraordinary activity of the organism would be without clinical proof? The reproductive organs must be deeply involved and this involvement must be ascertainable. Surely we cannot have the organs of generation working at high speed to supply the precious secretions without any noticeable signs. I am sure physiological evidence in plenteous measure would be available to the scientists who dedicate themselves to this research, provided the study is taken up in a serious manner, with due regard to the solemn nature and the colossal proportions of the problem.

It is impossible that an activity of this nature can occur without leaving unmistakable traces in the whole area of the human frame. There must occur definite variations in the microbiology of the system. The constant absorption of the generative fluids and hormones into the visceral organs and their ascent into the brain as an ultra-subtle life-essence cannot leave the blood and the cerebrospinal fluid unaffected. There must be definite signs of it present in both. In the case of those who are prone to ecstasy at intervals, the signs must be unmistakably present during the time the trance condition lasts, and even for some time later. The ductless gland system must also evince alteration in some way. In fact, once the position is grasped fully and groups of earnest, interested savants devote themselves to the investigation, a whole battery of tests might be devised to locate the activity and determine its course.

There are many cases of sudden arousal of the Serpent Power in the ashrams of India. Also we have many thousands practicing Yoga at various places in America and in Europe. In addition to this, there are, as I have said, hundreds, even thousands, of people who have spontaneous awakening of the power. Many of them are willing to be studied. There is thus a whole field ready for investigation. Contacts with other yogis in India, who have awakened the force, and clearly avowed this in their writings, can throw further light on the whole phenomenon, enabling intelligent investigators to develop effective methods or instruments for the research.

The first need is, however, a thorough documentary study and visit to Yoga centers and ashrams in India to gain a comprehensive knowledge of the mechanism. At the present stage, it seems unlikely that an enlightened consciousness could be distinguished from a normal one with the use of the current devices. If it is not possible to distinguish the undoubtedly extended consciousness of a great intellectual or genius, it would not be possible to do so in the case of an illuminatus either.

The confirmation can come subjectively from another individual in whom the power is awakened. With a thorough study, it is possible that some clues might be found to reveal the activity of the radiating bio-energy responsible for the extraordinary visionary experiences and the paranormal phenomena. If not now, at least in the very near future.

There are some mediums who experience orgiastic sensations during their séances and there is, at least, one good psychic healer who, working in trance state, swallows enormous quantities of alcohol, probably to replenish the energy consumed. There are intelligent men and women who, during spells of intense concentration on some piece of work or during meditation, feel erotic sensations in their genitals or have the sensation with visionary experiences. A probe directed into all such cases can bring forth, in the light of what has been stated, valuable data for a fully substantiated scientific investigation of the phenomenon.

With a little insight gained after the preliminary study and investigation, the sphere of research can be extended to include schizophrenics and manic-depressives, of whom most probably a large percentage represents the area of malfunctioning of the Serpent Power. The efforts of Kundalini, i.e., the evolutionary mechanism, extend to every sphere of human life. The extraordinarily intelligent, eloquent, and versatile men and women who rise to prominence or power in any field must have a stimulated Kundalini. They do not know it nor do the learned at this time. The safety and progress of mankind rests in the hands of these men and women and now, in the nuclear age, it is of utmost importance that the power behind their mental preeminence should become known. Apart from all these factors, the possibility, inherent in this investigation, should be a most powerful incentive for humane savants to take up the study, if for no other reason than at least to mitigate the horrors of a dreadful malady that has millions in its grip.

Needed: Talented Minds to Develop the World

I have yet much to reveal about this mighty mechanism, and this will be done in the course of time. This much I can say with confidence, that the eager rush for instant enlightenment, in which millions are zealously taking part today, though it may not lead to illumination in the majority of cases, will at least prepare the soil for a mass understanding of what I say, once the academic formalities have been completed. The awakening of the Truth is sure to come to millions with a little more experience in the methods they are pursuing. There is only one sublime goal for all mankind, though the paths leading to it might be different. Unless the goal is achieved, the mind never finds rest and the question still remains unanswered. Out of all the millions of honest seekers, sacrificing their time, energy, and resources in this sacred endeavor, those who find the answer will be the first to corroborate what I assert about the nature of true enlightenment. Until then I have the patience to wait. In all my writings, I have sown the seeds of what I consider to be the most pressing need of mankind, namely information about the evolutionary mechanism in human beings, slowly drawing the race to a golden future of harmony, peace, and happiness. I am not eager for an immediate success, for the future clearly looms before my vision in all its glory and charm. Some one or other will water the seeds and carry the investigation to a successful end. What was essential is that the disclosure should be broadcast, and heaven has graciously helped me to that end. The rest is a matter of time, for the destined hour for this knowledge has come.

It is the talented mind that, in the last analysis, is at the bottom of every situation that develops in the world. It is the men and women, endowed with extraordinary mental gifts, who shape the thinking of not only the masses but also of the elite who rule them. Therefore no one of them can exonerate himself or herself from responsibility, at least from the moral point of view, for the present highly inflammable condition of the world and the deplorable state of crowds of young men and women whom the evolutionary pressure has made or is making self-tormenting rebels to society.

It is an enigma to me why there should be an attitude of disbelief over what I am stating when all that I aver does not, in essentials, differ from what has been said by Freud and, with some modification, by Jung also. The only difference is that I ascribe the mystical experience and paranormal phenomena to the same agency which they hold responsible for the sexual behavior, extraordinary talents, and abnormal states of the human mind. I make the position even more concrete and trace the force to its somatic foundation, exposing its real nature and, for open-minded scientists, laying bare a channel through which empirical corroboration can come for the view expressed. There is, therefore, nothing in the concepts of modern psychology that I flout or destroy. On the other hand, I attempt to rescue it from the current highly detrimental and unwarrantedly materialistic bias. With proper investigation, the present explosive world situation, the enigmatic revolt of the youth, increase in crime and violence, the rising tide of mental disorders and drugs, as also the ardent search of millions for methods of self-transcendence or self-knowledge will all be traced to the activity of the evolutionary mechanism in human beings. I am as sure of it as I am of my own self. If what I assert is not proved by impartial time, I should go down to the progeny as a self-deluded and highly reprehensible being. Time alone will show how far I am right in what I have said.

III

Is Meditation Always Beneficial?
Some Positive and Negative Views

The present wave of interest in higher states of consciousness and in the exploration of the inner world, now sweeping America and Europe, has a deeper reason behind it than is usually understood by those engaged in the study of the human mind. This is not just a passing phase, a shifting of human interest from the material to the spiritual for a change, or just a vagary of the mind. It is based on the pressure of certain psychophysiological changes in the human nervous system and the brain to mark the point where consciousness finds itself in a position to turn its search on itself in order to unravel its own mystery.

The same phenomenon almost invariably occurred when a people in the past attained a certain level of civilization and—for the well-to-do classes at least—material amenities and leisure provided the occasion for this inner exploration. It happened in Sumer, Egypt, India, China, Greece, and other places. The record of what their research revealed, at least in part, still exists.

The reappearance of the same thirst in this age of reason is attended with problems which were not present before, however. It has to contend now with the dominating intellect and to convince it that this recrudescence is based on a pressing need of the human psyche and is not a mere chance intruder with which one could deal arbitrarily as one liked.

During this period of conflict—between this growing thirst for spiritual experience and the still skeptical ranks of rationalists—a certain amount of confusion is inevitable. There are many intellectuals who believe that the states of illumination which many thousands of people are seeking are but the inner mental states bordering on the subconscious. They hold that these states can be evoked in hypnosis or during the alpha and theta phases of biofeedback. "A yogi can learn to control his brain waves in a matter of years," say Karlins and Andrews in their work *Biofeedback,* adding that "the average person using biofeedback training can learn to control his brain waves in a matter of hours."

They quote Dr. Johann Stoyva as saying that information feedback techniques might be able to teach the "blank-mind" state, typical of Zen and Yoga, within "months or even weeks." Stoyva's own experience of alpha, they say, "was like a flowing gray-black film with a luminous quality." At another place: "As the technology for measuring and training brain waves becomes more sophisticated, unpracticed meditators will have the opportunity to duplicate the physiological states of Zen and Yoga."

This is a misconception. The gravity of the error lies not in misjudging the nature of mystical ecstasy and the phenomenon of illumination, closely associated with it, but in completely overlooking a factor which is of paramount importance for human welfare and safety. This is the factor of evolution or, in other words, of the resistless change in human consciousness, caused by an equally resistless, though still imperceptible, microbiological change in the human brain.

We see unchallengable evidence for this transformation when we compare the relics of ancient cultures, three to five thousand years old, with the culture of today. But as a group, biologists are not prepared to concede that the human brain is still in a process of organic evolution, for they see no perceptible symptoms of such a process. True, there are no discernible signs in the brain to attest to this transformation. But then are we able to decipher all the cryptic language of the cranium and is it not still almost a complete mystery to us?

Until very recently we could not even find any visible organic signs of such a glaring pathological upheaval as that of insanity, and even eminent psychologists believed it to be purely psychic in nature. Even now the biological origin of insanity is completely obscure. On what evidence then do the erudite pass their judgments, when the nature of the bio-energy and the microbiology of the brain are still a closed book? It seems that many of them are not exempt from that common human frailty of drawing hasty conclusions and spreading them abroad for their own edification.

The very first experience of the beatific state brings the realization home to one who has it that the nature of consciousness varies with different individuals. The difference between a blockhead and an intellectual is a difference in the depth and volume of the consciousness of each. Each point of awareness, representing a human being, has its own spectrum, its own brightness, depth, and volume and in this way each varies from the other. The consciousness of the enlightened person is virtually illuminated and he or she lives—both in the waking and dreaming states—in a resplendent world of light.

Consciousness is a sovereign reality of the universe. Its range of manifestations is infinite. Just as there are subhuman states of consciousness so there are also transhuman states. Mystical consciousness or enlightened awareness marks the lowest limit of the transhuman variety. There have been historical personages who had it either occasionally or as a perennial possession from birth.

We see this state of illumination gradually increasing when

we rise from the lowest to the highest strata of the human mind, both conscious and subconscious. The tragedy is that every individual is enclosed in a water-tight shell of his own mind and is entirely debarred from having even one fleeting glimpse of that of another. This strict isolation makes each individual invest others with the same kind of consciousness that he has himself, with more or less intelligence, sensitivity, etc. This is a fallacy.

There is a difference in the very structure or spectrum of each individual consciousness caused by the difference in the biological organism through which it is expressed. The very texture of illumined consciousness is thus distinct and different from others. It is not only that one has visual feasts of light and color or an extended awareness, but wholesale transformation of consciousness must occur.

During the course of a genuine mystical experience a higher dimension of consciousness intervenes, eclipsing the normal individuality, partially or wholly, for a certain period. It then seems as if a new world, a new order of existence, or a super-human being has descended into view. There is an unmistakably enhanced perception of lights, colors, beauty, goodness, virtue, and harmony which lend a superworldly appearance to the whole experience.

Do we not see this greater apperception of light, color, beauty, harmony, ideals, moral values, and creative joy in the great geniuses of mankind, the great painters, sculptors, musicians, writers, philosophers, poets, mystics, and reformers of both the past and present?

Transcendental consciousness, adorned with all these attributes, is but a step ahead and must be clearly understood as such to chart out the direction in which the evolution of consciousness is taking place before our very eyes. If it is possible to produce geniuses of all these catgories, with guided meditation, biofeedback training, drugs, hypnosis, letting the mind go, or other practices of that sort, then enlightenment cannot fail to respond to the same treatment to produce Christs, Buddhas, or Platos in lavish numbers in the years to come. If not, then why all this confusion?

Biofeedback and Mystical Experience

Biofeedback equipment is designed to identify certain phases of consciousness. The technique has come into use because some of the scientists who are experimenting on consciousness are under the impression that the alpha and theta states provide the matrix from which mystical experience and creative talent are born. It also provides an avenue for the cure of mental and even bodily ailments and for acquiring greater mastery over the mind.

By means of a signal, which can take the form of light or sound, biofeedback provides an index for identifying different stages of consciousness, namely, (1) alert wakefulness, (2) stilled, passive, relaxed, or vacant states, (3) the somnolent states preceding sleep, and (4) deep sleep. They are designated as beta, alpha, theta, and delta respectively. Alpha and Theta are slower-paced waves and are associated with inward attention, problem-solving, creativity, etc.

In order to point out the error involved in this supposition, it is necessary first of all to differentiate between the alpha and theta states and the state of concentrated attention that precedes the mystical ecstasy. According to the *Yoga Sutras* of Patanjali—and every other time-honored manual of Yoga—the mind has to pass through two stages of concentration, name dharana and dhyana, i.e., a primary state of concentration and a more stabilized and prolonged form of it. Only then can it attain to Samadhi or the mystical trance. There are detailed directions in all Yoga treatises on how this state of unbroken fixity of attention can be achieved. The target to be attained is that the observing mind and the object contemplated should fuse into one. This can occur in only two ways: Either the object dissolves into consciousness and only the seer remains intensely conscious of himself, or he loses his own identity and becomes one with the object on which the mind is fixed.

In fact, the rigorous forms of Pranayama, Mudras, and

Bhandas, peculiar to Hatha Yoga, are all aimed to enhance the effect of concentration on the brain and nervous system even further in order to accelerate the awakening of the Serpent Power. With gradual practice, the mind is trained to fall into deeply absorbed conditions which, in Samadhi, attain a depth that makes the seer oblivious to his surroundings though far more intensely aware within.

The aim of the practices is to keep only one object or one line of thought before the mind to the exclusion of every other object or chain of ideas. In order to achieve one-pointedness of the mind, a great deal of voluntary effort is necessary, and the practitioner has to keep himself always in a state of alertness to prevent his mind from slipping into passive or drowsy states or into other streams of thought and fancy. It is clear, therefore, that there is a world of difference between a passive, inwardly focused mental condition—where the ideas are allowed to meander and drift, as is the case in the state preceding sleep —and the alert, attentive, centrally focused state of mind necessary for concentration in all its forms.

This is clearly brought out in the Bhagavad Gita at various places. In verse 25 of the sixth discourse, for instance: "Little by little let him gain tranquility by means of reason, controlled by steadiness. Having made the mind abide in Self, let him not think of anything. . . . As often as the wavering and unsteady mind goeth forth, so often reining it in, let him bring it under the control of the self."

This point is further elucidated by Krishna in reply to the query of Arjuna, in which the latter points out that the mind is extremely restless and as hard to curb as the wind. "Without doubt, O might armed," says Krishna (VI.35), "The mind is hard to curb and restless, but it may be curbed by constant practice and by dispassion."

The cultivation of a one-pointed mind, as a prelude to attaining God-consciousness, is also repeatedly emphasized in the Upanishads. "Taking hold of the bow," says the Mundaka Upanishad (II.2, 3), "One should fix on it an arrow, sharpened with meditation. Drawing the string with a mind absorbed in the thought of Brahman hit, O good-looking one, that very target which is the Immutable."

The citations can be multiplied indefinitely to show that the practice of meditation, undertaken in all Yoga disciplines, has to be active in nature and that the mind has to be kept fully alert, focused only on one thought or image. The discipline is to be continued until the mind becomes habituated to concentrated application on one image or subject for prolonged periods. It is a well-known fact that this state of one-pointed attention and absorption is better developed in the highly intelligent and talented mind and is a prominent characteristic of every form of genius. On the other hand, the vacant, idiotic, and insane minds lack in the power to focus their attention intelligently on any subject for a sizable duration of time.

The irony is that some teachers of Yoga and other meditational techniques in America and Europe, by their own admissions and demonstrations, confirm this entirely erroneous view of the scholars and scientists, particularly in the United States. Those who declare certain kinds of Asanas or a certain amount of control over their respiration, heart action, and other metabolic processes to be Yoga or, in other words, the summum bonum of this time-honored discipline, fall into the very trap by which many of the western scholars are gripped at the moment.

There are others who prescribe negative forms of concentration, forbidden by the ancient masters, which allow the mind to think loosely or wander ceaselessly during meditation, leading to passive, somnolent, or quiescent states indicated by the alpha signal in biofeedback. They say that the visionary experiences or the creative flashes that sometimes occur in this state, as they do sometimes in dreams, also, are the landmarks of genuine mystical experience.

It is not, therefore, to be wondered that western scientists, misled by these annunciations of professional Yoga teachers, equate the transcendental state of mystical ecstasy with self-induced, quiescent, daydreaming, vacant, or passive states of the mind. In this assessment they fail to take notice of the fact that in all the descriptions of the mystical ecstasy there are certain very prominent and unmistakable symptoms that are not encountered in the alpha or the theta states. These are (1) vivid sensations of light both within and without, (2) a feeling of extreme rapture which is reflected in the whole appearance of the individual, (3) often streaming tears at the majestic and sublime nature of the spectacle, (4) a sense of intimacy or proximity to an infinite Presence or a celestial being, (5) contact with an infinite fount of knowledge, (6) horripilation, (7) a sense of unbounded wonder and awe at the surpassing vision, and (8) intellectual illumination with Jnana, i.e., perennial wisdom.

During the period the ecstasy lasts, the awareness is highly intensified and enlarged. The individual becomes more fully conscious within than he ever was before, and the impact of the experience is often so powerful that even one single excursion into this ineffable territory remains indelibly imprinted on the memory to serve as a landmark through the rest of life.

It is the memory of a glorious transhuman or otherworldly experience which is lived intensely for a brief duration—beyond the least shadow of doubt—and not of a dreamlike or visionary human state, however realistic and vivid it might have seemed at the time. The genuine mystical experience deals a shattering blow to the ego and melts down the walls that segregate the individual from the rest of his fellow beings.

The narcissistic and phoney forms of Yoga or other disciplines, on the contrary, inflate the ego even more and isolate even more completely the individual from the resplendent One in All. This is the reason why the truly illuminated are humble, unpretentious, and childlike in their behavior, indifferent to worldly greatness and fame. While, on the contrary, unenlightened professional spiritual teachers are often self-centered, dominating, and ostentatious, eager for a following and the adulation of crowds. In one breathless moment of inner illumination, wrought by the successful practice of Yoga, the whole personality of a man can undergo a radical change for life. "He who is happy within, who rejoiceth within, who is illuminated within," says the Bhagavad Gita (5.24), "that Yogi, becoming the Eternal, goeth to the Peace of the Eternal."

In raising these issues I do not want to cast any doubt about the therapeutic value of biofeedback training or of hypnosis or of those systems of Yoga and methods of mind-culture which prescribe passive, empty, or fluidic states of mind for the practice of meditation. Nor do I want to raise questions about their capacity to bestow calm and relaxed states of mind or even to induce visionary or extrasensory states with weird features and colors, like the ones described by the scientists engaged in this investigation. But this weird or exotic imagery, color, shape, or feature—unattended by other symptoms—is not mystical experience at all. We sometimes have the same experiences even in dreams or with drugs, and they do not signify the beatific state nor a contact with Cosmic Consciousness. When once this fact is clearly grasped then only can there be any hope of a well-directed investigation into the still little-understood mystical ecstasy and other allied phenomena.

Mystical Consciousness Vs. Drug States

Other eminent psychic researchers equate mystical ecstasy with LSD experiences and the hypnotic state. They assert openly that the LSD state is very similar to mystical experience or that they can induce the mystical trance into their hypnotized subjects with proper suggestions. It is easy to see that this trend in the present-day thinking of scientists engaged in consciousness research is fatal to the lofty ideals of religion and, with one stroke of the pen, reduces the sublime nature of mystical ecstasy to the level of mere mundane experiences possible in sleep, in passive, semiconscious states, or inducible with drugs, hypnotic suggestion, and other techniques.

If these mistaken ideas are allowed to spread unquestioned, they are likely to rob religion of all its divine color and reduce it to the babblings of individuals prone to delusory states of mind with drugs, autohypnosis, or promptings from the subconscious in relaxed or semiawake states between wakefulness and deep sleep.

An enterprising writer, R. Gordon Wasson, has identified the Soma of the Vedas—the drink of gods, which bestowed immortality and led to ecstasy and highest inspirational states —with the mushroom *Amanita muscaria*, or fly agaric in English. This brilliant red mushroom with white spots is said to be familiar in forests and folklore throughout northern Eurasia. The juice crushed out of the mushroom, the author believes, was used by Vedic seers copiously as an inebriant, and it is this Soma juice which is lavishly mentioned in various hymns as the source of inspiration of the Vedic poets. "The most astonishing of candidates for Soma was exposed by Sir Aural Stein, the explorer-scholar, as Rhubarb," says Wasson. "According to Stein himself, no Indian in recorded history has made a fermented drink of Rhubarb, though of course, with the addition of sugar or honey the juice lends itself to fermentation. Stein must have forgotten either his Rig Veda or his sense of humor."

Wasson further says that in 1921 an Indian had advanced the notion that Soma, after all, was nothing but Bhang, the Indian name of marijuana, cannabis sativa, or hemp, hashish. In a flash of illumination, he now replaces both of these with a "mushroom."

How far Wasson's own opinion is worth credence will be clear when it is pointed out that Soma is also the name of the moon, which is associated with the luster in the head created by Kundalini. In every depiction of Lord Shiva, the crescent of the moon is shown invariably on one side of the head. The Vedic hymns, when read with clear knowledge about Kundalini, show plainly that the drink of immortality is the ambrosia mentioned in the Tantras and books on Yoga, whether Indian, Tibetan, or Chinese.

This nectarean substance flows into the head (as a radiant, living energy) and then circulates in the body on the arousal of Kundalini. The Vedic hymns clearly mention the attendant signs of thunder, light, and sounds, the symbology of the bull, sky, and the nectar; also the moods of ecstasy and inspiration which characterize the ascent of the serpent fire into the brain.

There must have been a fermented drink too, used as a stimulant even by the priests, just as we have alcohol today. But no priest or divine or other ecclesiastic of our time has waxed eloquent about it as the bestower of immortality and the vision of gods.

Lack of knowledge about the phenomenon of Kundalini, and ignorance of the fact that it has been at the base of the religious and magical practices and concepts of antiquity, have been responsible for causing enormous confusion among the scholars in interpreting the ancient texts. We have similar symbology in Tantras also where the word "wine" is mentioned with a double meaning. It is the common beverage often used in Tantric worship and also the drink of divine intoxication, poured by an awakened Kundalini into the brain to cause the most intense rapture and bliss which is characteristic of the ecstatic state.

Wasson himself seems to have forgotten to draw the correct inference from the hymn in the Rig Veda (X. 85.3), which says, "One thinks one drinks Soma because a plant is crushed. The Soma that the Brahmans know—that no one drinks." Brahmans means the knowers of Brahman or Cosmic Consciousness. Can there be any doubt that the word "soma" has an esoteric meaning also? It refers to that vitalizing internal beverage—with unlimited power of rapture—which nature has provided as an incentive to the evolutionary effort in the same way as it has provided the transport of love as the incentive for the equally important procreative act of man.

In Sufi poetry there is the same play on the words "grape" and "wine." The Taoists call it the "Elixir," the Indian alchemists "parada" or "mercury." Dr. Mircea Eliade has made a similar error in regard to the "nectar" which is said to drip down the throat from the palate with Khecheri Mudra and holds it to be saliva, implying that the ancient masters, who show such a deep knowledge of human anatomy, had not the acumen to make a distinction between saliva and the flow of an exhilarating essence in the region specified.

A similar error has been made by C. G. Jung in his *Psy-*

chology of the Unconscious in interpreting a Vedic hymn, referring to the fire produced by the friction of two sticks. He treats it as an allusion to coition, while the terms used clearly point to the fire produced by Kundalini. Meanwhile, what has already been stated is enough to show that lack of sufficient knowledge of the esoteric aspects of ancient religions can ensnare even the most powerful intellect—not initiated into the mystery—into drawing wholly erroneous conclusions.

If the present-day trends in science continue to grow, the day is not distant when the state of religion in the countries that still follow some kind of faith would be no better than what it is now in communist lands. It will reduce the precious spiritual heritage of humankind—the Bible, the Upanishads, the Bhagavad Gita, the Quran, the Discourses of the Buddha, and the inspired utterances of other saints and mystics of all lands —both in importance and value and deprive all the lofty ideals of their grandeur and worth. The very fact that the existing major faiths almost everywhere have been a most dominating factor in the life of mankind for the past thousands of years should make the scholars pause and consider that there must be some inexplicable reason at the bottom: What made vast multitudes accept their sway for such long periods of time and still do the same even in this rational age, in spite of all the apathy and even antagonism of sundry luminaries of science?

This point must be made with some force because of the momentous issues involved. The various systems of Yoga are designed to accelerate the evolutionary changes occurring in the human body, to raise the brain to a supersensory level of cognition. In fact, this is the natural aim of all healthy religious disciplines and practices. The whole fabric of religion—its beliefs, tenets, rituals, and practices—owes its existence to the instinctive response of surface consciousness to the demand of the evolutionary impulse, operating in the deepest recesses of the human psyche. It is, therefore, obvious that any practice or discipline, designed to lead to a more evolved state of consciousness, must conform in essentials to the means used by nature for effecting this transformation.

The main factor responsible for the mental evolution of mankind from remote periods to the present day, and even now operating to keep evolutionary trends active, is not hard to understand. Whatever progress has been achieved so far in art, science, philosophy, music, painting, sculpture, or technology—in short, in every known branch of knowledge and skill—has been gained by dint of rigorous mental effort-study, reflection, and concentration of mind. Steady application of the mind, done voluntarily in full wakefulness day by day by countless men and women, has made mankind what it is today. Is there one single man or woman of talent who rose to distinction without herculean effort?

Meditational Tricks and True Illumination

It is remarkable to what extent the learned can be led astray by their own prepossessions or faulty ways of thought. Spiritual genius is as much a higher faculty of the mind as any other form of genius and talent. If constant application and ceaseless endeavor are essential prerequisites for the culture of mind and the expression of genius in all other branchs of knowledge, can it be conceived even for a moment that religious genius forms the one single exception to this general rule? Can deep spiritual insights and sublime experiences be gained by allowing the mind to wander and sink into semiawake states in which active effort is completely ruled out?

Is there any historical record to show that the most honored spiritual guides of mankind—Socrates, Christ, Vyasa, Buddha, Shankara, St. Paul, Kabir, Rumi, and others—were not intensely alert and wakeful throughout their lives and that they mumbled their teachings in half-awake or semiconscious states with a stilled mind withdrawn from active thought? Either mankind has been in error throughout the past in resorting to ceaseless voluntary mental application to gain knowledge and to resolve its problems or there is something radically wrong with the thinking of today's savants, who equate absent-minded and semiawake mental states, evoked with the use of biofeedback or other means, with genuine mystical experience or even the creative moods of gifted minds.

Those who express these views have no idea of the damage they cause in the thinking of the general public, which relies on them for guidance. There is already a tendency to shirk the effort necessary for constructive thinking and, not unoften, individuals of this category assimilate only the predigested ideas of other people. Too much recourse to passive mental states—daydreaming, mind-wandering, stillness, quietude, or vacuity of thought—provides easy ways of escape for millions from facing the hard realities of life. "There is no expedient to which a man will not go to avoid the real labor of thinking," says Thomas Edison. We see this happening every day—the well-conducted publicity or advertising campaign to successfully popularize a product, idea, or personality.

Man is still in a state of transition from the normal to transhuman consciousness. In this respect, he is like a child still in the process of growth. For the development of a child's mind do its parents or teachers ever advise it to let its mind wander while attending to the lesson, or is the greatest stress laid on undivided attention? What error in thinking then makes us catch frantically at cheap, spurious methods to gain enlightenment?

These methods provide no avenue for success in Yoga. Just as no one can become an athlete by idleness or passive states of the body, so no one can gain access to higher levels of consciousness with idleness or passive states of the mind. What is needed is intense application, alternating with needful periods of rest in the right proportion. This is what the Bhagavad Gita emphasizes when it says that Yoga is only for one who is regulated in sleep and wakefulness.

The passive methods of meditation that lead to stillness or semiawake states and the mental conditions evoked by biofeedback practices are but disguised variations of the famous formula of the well-known French psychiatrist, Émile Coué, "I am getting better and better every day in every way," repeated in the quiescent state preceding sleep.

Passive states of mind provide rest from tension and can, no doubt, have a curative and calming effect in a tense environment caused by today's complex life. But then, like sleep and hypnosis, they should be plainly labeled as such and not acclaimed as substitutes for Yoga or other active spiritual disciplines which are designed to lead to extended states of consciousness. The moment this is done they become stumbling blocks in the path of those who have the environment, the time, and the capacity to strive for mastery in the art of concentration.

The alpha and theta states are the very antithesis of the attentive or concentrated states of mind essential for the evolution of the brain. They have their own value for rest, release, and relaxation, but there can be no greater blunder than to pass them off as illuminative or creative states, which depend on a certain peculiar constitution of the brain and nervous system.

The highly attentive state of mind of a greater writer or thinker, an astronomer, or a psychologist, deeply absorbed in his work, is not the passive, quiescent, vacant, or semiawake condition represented by the Alpha or Theta waves. It is a state of effortless concentration, matured with practice, in which the mind remains actively engaged all the time. From this state one can pass quietly into Samadhi, with the consciousness now contemplating itself, in place of the object contemplated, in all its glory and unbounded expanse.

There is a difference only of degree between the brain of a great intellectual and an enlightened mystic. Hence an illuminated consciousness can never be attained with a meditational trick or magical device or the miraculous gift of a saint. It needs the same hard labor and hereditary predisposition as any other extraordinary faculty of the mind.

It is by far easier for a talented mind to become illuminated than for that of a man of low intelligence. This possibility has been fully recognized by the Indian masters. Spontaneous flashes of illumination occur mainly in individuals of the former class, and they can win to the unitive state with comparatively less effort with jnana (discriminative knowledge), karma (selfless action), and bhakti (devotion), if they model their lives and keep their minds in constant calm reflection on the Divine.

The methods enjoined by all great founders of religions—devotional prayer, worship, constant thought on the Deity, devout daily meditation, and the like—with a harmonized life and noble traits of character, are far more efficacious in leading to the beatific state than most of the modern methods widely in use today. There is no way to cross the border that separates the transcendental from the mundane, save with the methods prescribed by revelation, and by acting on the basic principles common to all revealed religions of mankind.

Cultivation of Sustained Attention Leads to Yoga

The dispersed, drifting, or semiawake condition of mind is not the inwardly focused state of a true mystic or awakened seer. The stillness of this state, in the words of D. A. Baker, the Benedictine mystic, "is the stillness of the soaring eagle which cleaves its way through the blue with motionless wings. It is the rest that springs from an unusually large amount of actualized energy, the rest that is produced by action, unperceived because so fleet, so near, so all-fulfilling."

The ultimate state in Yoga, namely Samadhi, is a state of equipoise and calm, of stillness and beatitude brought about by a tremendously enhanced awareness which soars beyond the regions fed by the senses and the mind. It is not a semiconscious but a superconscious state in which the interior of man becomes lustrous like the sun, and the dancing beams of consciousness penetrate to regions forever shut out from the sight of those who have not attained the finished state of the brain indispensable for illumination.

The point to be emphasized particularly is that, in dealing with the paranormal and transcendental, we have to distinguish between the states brought about by two distinct methods of approach to the occult and the divine. One is by the cultivation of attention to the point which is inherently present in almost all exceptionally talented minds, where it can remain calmly focused on an object or subject for prolonged periods of time, without visible effort or strain. Other ideas or even mild external impressions coming through the senses are excluded. This is the power of absorbed attention characteristic of a Newton or an Einstein or other great prodigies of knowledge and intellect.

This power of sustained attention can be cultivated by voluntary effort. All healthy methods of Yoga are designed to this end. An accomplished yogi must gain the ability to maintain unbroken continuity of absorbed attention easily, in the same way as an expert cyclist or swimmer gains the ability to manipulate his machine or to stay afloat easily without visible effort. "With the mind not wandering after aught else, harmonized by continual practice, constantly meditating, O Partha," says the Bhagavad Gita (8.8), "One goeth to the spirit, Supreme, Divine." In this process there occur certain biological changes in the brain which it is not necessary to discuss in detail here. This biological perfection is already present in the brain of the man of genius, the towering intellectual, and the born mystic.

The other method is that of voluntary descent into the subconscious by means of autohypnosis, passive forms of meditation, vacuity of thought, allowing the mind to roam or with deliberately effected fatigue of the optic or auditory nerves. There are hundreds of methods in use in India, Tibet, and China for creating these passive, somnolent, vacant, or visionary states. The practitioners, coming across vivid visionary experiences or face to face with weird spectacles presented by the subconscious, in their ignorance, often accept them as signs of spiritual awakening, which actually is far from the case.

For instance, some of the Sadhakas in India and other places are asked to gaze fixedly on certain complicated diagrams which fascinate and, at the same time, bewilder the mind, such as a mandala of intersecting triangles and circles, or on a drop of ink on the thumbnail, or on certain sounds, like the mantra

"Aum," or on one's reflection in a mirror, especially of the eyes, with a relaxed, roaming or passive state of the mind.

In other cases they look fixedly at a black circle, hung on a wall, or at the sky or just watch, like a spectator, the flow of the drifting stream of thought or imagine vibrations of power coming from their preceptor, etc. The thoughts are often allowed to flow without restraint in whatever direction they choose. The outcome is obvious. In many cases, after varying intervals, a trance or semiawake condition supervenes. The practitioners begin to have extraordinary visionary experiences, like the ones described by those practicing autogenic methods or passive or blank-mind forms of meditation. But this condition is far from enlightenment, as far as the North Pole is from the South.

These are the very same methods and the very devices used by modern hypnotists to cause the somnambulistic trance in their subjects. They use revolving mirrors, scintillating lights, crystal balls, quaint geometrical designs, various swings, enigmatic figures, monotonous sounds, or weird music, with passive mental conditions, to bring about the hypnotic state. Where lies the difference if, instead of gazing into the eyes of a hypnotist one looks into the reflection of one's own eyes in a mirror or the eyes of a partner, seeking the same condition of mind?

What the subconscious holds we often come across in dreams or under the influence of drugs, which blunt or disfigure the surface consciousness. What mystical ecstasy reveals is a surpassing state of awareness which transcends both the conscious and the subconscious mind, revealing the universe in a new light never experienced before.

It is surprising how suggestible even the highly intelligent and erudite can be. Their learning or intellectual acumen cannot protect them from falling victim to the inherent tendencies of their minds. They fail to realize when a spiritual teacher—after expounding a certain method of mental discipline or control—says that, with practice, they would soon see strange sights or have unique experiences, that he is planting a suggestion which will bear fruit one day.

It is not surprising, therefore, that some people treat the enlightened state and the hypnotic trance as identical. If continued for prolonged periods on a mass scale, the effect of these practices is actually regressive and anti-evolutionary, in fact, The mental stagnancy that kept the once spiritually advanced people of India and other places tied to erroneous ideas and beliefs for centuries, until they were rescued from the rut by the spread of knowledge in recent times, has been in some measure due to these negative and anti-evolutionary practices.

It is characteristic of the evolutionary impulse, operating in the race, that a highly intelligent mind or, say, a more evolved consciousness, seeks a way of escape from the rational prison-house formed by the senses and the intellect. The natural way to satisfy this hunger for a greater measure of freedom for the spirit is to awaken the dormant forces in the body already provided by nature in order to effect the necessary transformation of the brain. The most effective methods to achieve this are the same as ordained by nature for gaining perfection in every branch of knowledge and skill—persistent mental application, study, and practice done in a healthy way. These methods, when applied to mind and consciousness, lead to that intuitive state which has provided the fountainhead for all the metaphysical and spiritual knowledge gained by mankind.

The use of methods for descent into the subconscious, to have otherworldly experiences, can be traced to remote periods of history. These methods have almost invariably been an adjunct to the religious practices of primitive people. They have also been used for magic, witchcraft, sorcery, and necromancy. It is unfortunate that many of the dedicated scientists now engaged on this investigation have not yet been able to make a distinction between these two mutually antagonistic methods of approach to the transcendental.

The use of these practices to reach the subconscious for weird or even pleasing experiences never produced a great genius or an illumined seer. Had this kind of meditation and mind-culture been in accordance with the natural tendencies of the human psyche, then it is on the ancient highlands of Tibet or the fertile plains of India and China that the crop of geniuses, which flourished in Europe and America in the eighteenth and nineteenth centuries, would have been born. Then India would never have ceased to produce a recurring crop of spiritual geniuses and enlightened seers who illuminated the Upanishadic period. That this did not come to pass is a clear testimony to the fact that there was something amiss in the social organization, life, thinking, and religious practices that followed the ascendant period of the Vedic age.

The gullibility, inertia, or ignorance of modern scholars, in this sphere of vital importance for the progress and safety of the race, is at the bottom of all this confusion. Science has so far been concerned mainly with discovering the laws ruling the material universe and the biological frame of man. Through its efforts, mankind has now attained to an intellectual height where it is imperative for it to know the laws of its evolving mind and consciousness. This needs as deep and prolonged a study of the phenomenon as has been devoted to other fields of knowledge during the past two hundred years.

The present arbitrary and unsystematic methods, directed toward understanding the nature of mystical ecstasy and the evolutionary target of the human mind, like biofeedback, hypnosis, drugs, and the rest, can only be considered as leaps in darkness from a summit, surrounded by abysmal depths on every side.

The object of the evolutionary process is to release the self-conscious mind of man more and more from the thraldom of the subconscious to enable it to touch levels of cognition which, in its present fettered condition, it can never reach. Just as a man awakening from a frightful dream returns to his normal state with a deep sense of relief and gratitude, in the same way the awakened seeker contemplates, with joy and thankfulness, the newly attained transcendent state of being, released from the cramping prison-cell of the sensory world. This process of release is considerably retarded when the conscious mind fails to assert itself and tamely submits to the dictates of the subconscious.

Spiritual evolution does not imply a greater skill in penetrating to below-the-surface regions of the human mind but in raising it to levels of perception which it never.possessed before. It is to this enhanced perception of gifted minds that all progress of mankind has been due.

The gravest distempers of modern civilization owe their existence to the deplorable lack of healthy methods of mind-culture and character building to conform to the evolutionary processes active within. Formerly, to some extent, religion provided this vital need. But now a new orientation is necessary. The individuals, born with extended consciousness and exceptional intelligence, are thus cast adrift in a world entirely oblivious to the need for psychophysiological disciplines, necessary to keep pace with the inner development.

The alarming increase in the number of drug addicts, alcoholics, chain-smokers, hysterics, delinquents, anarchists, idlers, and rebels to society, leading to a no less alarming increase in mental disorders, crime, and violence, is an unavoidable outcome of this grave neglect.

If humanity is to be saved from disaster, voluntary mind-culture and character building, as a preparation for the emergence of higher consciousness—at least in the case of individuals genetically ripe for the development—should form an integral part of all educational systems, just as physical exercise and hygiene do today.

The day is not distant when, with the realization of the irresistible evolutionary trends in the human body, the elite would be compelled to bow submissively to this imperious demand of the evolving human brain, drawing mankind toward a glorious pre-allotted destination.

The inextinguishable spark of inquiry in man will never rest content until it finds an answer to its own problems. The answer can never come from the intellect, which is already tottering under the weight of the knowledge it has so far gathered. But the answer will come through a superior channel of paranormal perception which mankind must develop to fulfill its destiny.

The whole fabric of human life, its social, political, religious, and educational structures will have to be remodeled to meet this need. The culture of mind and moral rearmament are the two most essential ingredients in this inescapable readjustment. Mankind is face to face now with the most critical situation in its evolutionary career, a situation that needs calm reflection, study, and research and not the haphazard expedients we are adopting at the moment.

IV

The Goal of Meditation

A mind intensely concentrated on one single object is like a pinioned bird that cannot move its head. In this condition it can only see the object immediately before its eyes. There is then absolutely no possibility of its soaring in ever-widening circles to infinity. A state of abstraction like that of a mathematician solving a problem, or a painter drawing a likeness, is actually what is needed to be cultivated. An arrowmaker, so engrossed in his work that he fails to see the king passing by, is a classical example mentioned in Indian treatises.

The aim of concentration is to stimulate a dormant reservoir of psychic energy to feed the brain. Mere pinpointing of the mind in itself is not illumination. It is only when there is a flow of this energy to the brain that the mind can slip its tether of the body and observe its transformation into an oceanic entity with amazement and awe.

The sensation of light or fire or inner illumination is a distinctive sign of the flow of this psychic force. The intellect continues to function in the background, as otherwise how can the condition be assessed and described? This is clearly mentioned in the Indian scriptures. If intense concentration or pinpointing of the mind were an indispensable precondition, then other forms of Yoga—as for instance the Yoga of selfless action, or devotion and intellectual discrimination (the "wisdom of Plato")—would be entirely ineffective in inducing the mystical state.

In that case, how can we account for the experiences of those who have sporadic flashes of illumination? There is a whole army of talented men and women who, without any regular spiritual discipline or practice of Yoga, had the experience thrust upon them in a way that left a permanent mark on the whole course of their lives. The impact of the experience was so powerful that it outshone other extraordinary incidents of their lives. They include outstanding scientists and scholars about whose acuteness of perception and accuracy of observation there cannot be the least shadow of doubt.

They include such eminent figures as Pascal, Tennyson, Wordsworth, Charlotte Brontë, Walt Whitman, Richard M. Bucke, George Eliot, D. H. Lawrence, Nietzsche, and many others. Their descriptions of the extraordinary state possess certain features which, for one who has had the experience himself, at once affixes the seal of authenticity on their experiences.

A few sentences from three or four such cases would clarify what I mean. "I was in a state of quiet, almost passive enjoyment, not actually thinking, but letting ideas, images, and emotions flow of themselves, as it were, through my mind," says Bucke. "All at once, without warning of any kind, I found myself wrapped in a flame-colored cloud. For an instant I thought of fire. . . . Directly afterward, there came upon me a sense of exultation, of immense joyousness, accompanied or immediately followed by an intellectual illumination impossible to describe. . . . I saw that the universe is not composed of dead matter but is, on the contrary, a living Presence. . . ."

The experience of Arthur Koestler is somewhat different, but clearly refers to the same, sudden transformation of consciousness: "This cliché had an unexpectedly strong effect. I saw Einstein's world-shaking formula, Energy equals Mass multiplied by the square of the velocity of light, hovering in a kind of rarified haze over the glaciers, and this image carried a sensation of infinite tranquility and peace. . . . The sensation of choking with indignation was succeeded by the relaxed quietude and self-dissolving stillness of the oceanic feeling."

The version of Nietzsche seems even different but, on closer scrutiny, conveys the same significance and points to the same enlargement of consciousness. "Has anyone ever observed that music emancipates the spirit, gives wings to thought? . . . The grey sky of abstraction seems thrilled by flashes of lightning; the light is strong enough to reveal all the details of things; to enable one to grapple with problems, and the world is surveyed as if from a mountain top. . . . And unexpectedly answers drop into my lap, a small hailstorm of ice and wisdom, of problems solved. Where am I?"

This expanded consciousness does not only come with a sense of bliss, of stillness and peace, an oceanic feeling or the awareness of an infinite Presence, but many times with problems solved and riddles answered. It has come through history and will continue to come to the end of time with new masterpieces of music, poetry, and art, new discoveries of science and new horizons of philosophic thought.

It is a mistake to isolate mystical experience from the creative impulses of the human mind. The human consciousness is growing in an ever-widening circle and, in this process, continues to pour into the lap of humanity all that is precious in literature, art, and science. Every high intellectual and every genius, gifted with creativity, is very close to the border from which the mystical province begins. The vision and the experience can come at any time.

The main hindrance is one's own antagonistic frame of mind. All the systems of Yoga in India and every form of religious discipline, worship, or prayer is designed to overcome the barriers posed by the overcritical intellect, by dogma, skepticism, ego, pride, and other recalcitrant traits of the mind.

There are also other misconceptions about the beatific state. For instance, about the reality of time. "A third mark of almost all mystical metaphysics," says Bertrand Russell, "is the denial of the reality of time. This is an outcome of the denial of division; if all is one, the distinction of past and future must be illusory."

It is a serious error to deny the reality of time or space or, in other words, of the visible universe on the basis of mystical experience. No sensible astronaut would deny the reality of the environment met on earth on the basis of his experience in outer space. Such a frame of mind would be disastrous for his own safety. In the mystical trance, what is perceived is the world of life and consciousness. It is a different proposition from the world of phenomena. Therefore, what is witnessed there cannot be applied word for word to the outer world.

This frame of mind has often led to that apathy toward the problems of life which held many intelligent people in an iron grip until modern science came to demonstrate the enormous potentialities present in matter to shape the life of mankind. The mystic who would ignore the basic demands of his body in the transport of his entrancing experience would, after a time, not only lose the rapture but maybe his life also.

Loss of the sense of time also occurs in the exciting play of love, in sleep and dreams, while watching an absorbing scene or listening to music or when engrossed in creative work. Lovers meeting clandestinely see hours pass as if they had no duration, while half-an-hour's wait appears to be an age.

In the mystical trance the sense of time is lost because of the intensity of the experience and the timeless nature of consciousness itself. The same can happen to a lesser degree when reading an absorbing book or listening to a breathless tale narrated by an accomplished storyteller. In perennial ecstasy, the existence of the temporal world continues in the background of a timeless Presence. If it were not so, there is no possibility of a further evolution of consciousness to the mystical stage.

Genuine Samadhi or transcendental experience is like step-
ping into a wonderland where consciousness itself, and not the
sensual world, becomes the fascinating object of contemplation.
The mind and the intellect are immovably held in the observation of a breathtaking display that is beyond anything experienced on earth, even in dreams. Mark the words of Tennyson
when he says, "I felt my soul grown mighty and my spirit with
such a vast circumference of thought. . . ."

The only key to the understanding of mystical consciousness
lies in treating the phenomenon as a metamorphosis in the
cognitive capacity of the observer. The soul grows mighty and
the mental eye is immensely enlarged. When the mind of an
enlightened being is turned inward, the panorama that meets
his inner eye is of a colossal world of life that dwarfs the image
of the external world—present in his imagination—into insignificance. What is experienced is a living Presence, an inexpressible ocean of consciousness spread everywhere. The world
image seems to float like a reflection in a mirror, occupying but
a small portion of its unbounded periphery.

This is also true of the mystical state with visionary experiences. The image of God or Deity, perceived in the vision, is
not just an earthly image, ensconced in space and time, but
something superearthly and divine, immanent and majestic,
which gathers shape and form because of the visionary's own
highly expanded consciousness. In other words, the vision is a
projection of the mystic's consciousness itself.

What I wish to emphasize is the fact that mystical consciousness—whether of a sporadic nature or a permanent feature of
one's personality—is not the average or common state of human
awareness. Even if the motion of thought is stilled by the practice of any discipline, the dimension of the observing consciousness is not materially affected. This is also admitted by Patanjali, author of the *Yoga Sutras.*

So long as the distinction between the subject and the object
of contemplation continues to exist, the real experience of
Samadhi does not occur. The subject and the object must become one and consciousness recoil on itself, leading to a new

area of perception never experienced before. "The self, harmonised by yoga, seeth the Self abiding in all beings, all beings in the Self, everywhere he seeth the same," says the Bhagavad Gita (6.29). There is no ambivalence in this statement. The implication is clear beyond doubt. The ultimate aim of Yoga is to create a consciousness which sees the visible world in a new light, not as something alien or foreign to it, but as an inseparable part of itself. This clearly indicates a metamorphosis of the observer.

In looking at the objects around him, he now sees something new that he never observed before. He perceives the difference in the forms, the temporal durations, and the distances as distinctly as he did formerly, perhaps even more distinct than he did before. But at the same time, he sees all these things strung on consciousness as the pearls of a necklace are strung on a thread that runs through them all. Consciousness now becomes the primordial reality for the mystic in the waking, dream, and trance states. This is the reason why all authorities on higher states of consciousness in India agree on the point that Turiya—the transcendental state—covers all the other states of consciousness.

The enlightened consciousness which sees the divine in every object and every nook and corner of the universe, therefore, does not lose the sense of form but perceives everything distinctly as before. On the contrary, another faculty is added to the mind which enables it to perceive what it never saw before: the throbbing world of life, of inexpressible streams of consciousness flowing on all sides, like the transparent waters of a pellucid lake which allows the numerous aquatic creatures and plants, subsisting under its surface, to become distinctly visible without the least aberration in their forms. The sense of awe and wonder, of a fulfilling experience, of unbounded joy and the conviction of immortality, flows from this breathtaking transformation witnessed in oneself.

Wherever the enlightened consciousness looks it sees a projection of itself, diversified into the countless objects it beholds. But this is not all. When the external contacts are excluded and the consciousness broods on itself, it soon slips the anchor of the body and, extending in lustrous waves of undifferentiated awareness, assumes the proportion of a boundless ocean in which the melted ego retains just enough individuality to feel itself one with a stupendous universe of being that has no beginning and no end.

The present confusion among teachers of Yoga and some scientists arises from the fact that mystical experience has not been studied in the same methodical way as any other mysterious physical phenomenon. Too much reliance is being placed on the versions of some of the modern authors who pose as mystics without actually having had the true mystical experience. Few present-day investigators have any correct ideas about the topography of the province they are exploring. Almost every investigator has his own views about it and tries to find corroborative evidence to show that he is right. This is the very antithesis of what a correct approach to the numinous should be.

The intellect should present a clean slate of itself, for here we deal with those areas of creation that are beyond the probe of reason. This would eliminate the possibility of hasty and rash judgments as has been the position during recent years.

For instance, consider this statement of Aldous Huxley: "It will come about as the result of biochemical discoveries that will make it possible for large numbers of men and women to achieve a radical self-transcendence and a deeper understanding of the nature of things. And this revival of religion will be at the same time a revolution. From being an activity mainly concerned with symbols, religion would be transformed into an activity concerned mainly with experience and intuition— and everyday Mysticism underlying and giving significance to everyday rationality, everyday tasks and duties, everyday human relationships."

The obvious inference is that the use of biochemical reagents, or drugs, would make it possible for human beings to have a taste of mystical experience. Nothing can be more misleading and nothing further from the truth. There is no doubt that

mystical consciousness implies essentially a biological transformation of the brain, but this transformation is the same
kind as the conception and growth of an embryo.

The human child, no doubt, comes into being as a result of
certain biochemical processes, but are we in a position to fashion it without the agency of the human seed? The transformation of the brain, leading to transcendental consciousness,
needs the superintelligent, guiding touch of the living force
that is at the basis of all phenomena of life.

It is *this mysterious element in the human seed* which is
reponsible for all the storm of activity that takes place in the
womb. It is a cosmic medium that no human ingenuity can
ever create. Coming from the pens of popular writers, statements like that of Huxley have done great harm to the investigation of mystical phenomenon by depicting it as an alteration
of consciousness possible with drugs.

"The creative element in the mind of man, that latency
which can conceive gods, carve statues, move the heart within
the symbols of great poetry, or devise formulas of modern
physics," says Loren Eiseley, "emerges in as mysterious a fashion
as those elementary particles which leap into momentary existence in great cyclotrons, only to vanish again like infinitesimal
ghosts. The reality we know in our limited lifetime is dwarfed
by the unseen potential of the abyss where science stops."

The genuine mystical state marks a change in depth of the
whole human personality and the development of a new
supersensory organ of perception, known from immemorial
times by diverse names, like the Third Eye, the Sixth Sense,
the Eye of Wisdom, Divine Vision, and the rest.

"Since the development of life means the rise and growth
of consciousness," says Teilhard de Chardin, "that development
could not continue indefinitely along its own line without a
transformation in depth: like all great developments in the
world."

It is a superficial knowledge of mystical experience that can
believe that superficial methods, such as drugs, hypnosis,
guided meditation, mantras, or passive sleeplike states of mind

can lead to enlightenment. Mystical experience, even when sporadic, denotes a leap into a wider dimension of consciousness, which is the evolutionary target of the human race.

"If God and the human soul were completely different, no amount of logical reasoning or meditation could lead us to the reality of God," says Radhakrishnan. "God-consciousness is as much an original endowment of human beings as self-consciousness. There are degrees of God-consciousness as there are degrees of self-consciousness. In many men it is dim and confused; only in the redeemed soul is it completely manifest."

In mystical experience, therefore, we witness a new variety of consciousness which is absolutely unpicturable by those who have not experienced it one time or the other. "Everything that we can directly observe of the physical world happens inside our heads and consists of mental events in at least one sense of the word mental," says Bertrand Russell. "It also consists of events which form the part of the physical world. The development of this point of view will lead us to the conclusion that the distinction between mind and matter is illusory. The stuff of the world may be called physical or mental or both or neither as we please; in fact, the words serve no purpose."

In perennial mystical consciousness, the position of the subject and object remains the same, with this difference: that subjective consciousness now dominates the scene.

The differentiation of form, whatever its physical basis—from the point of view of our mental processes—depends primarily on the potentiality of consciousness to assume multifarious forms to interpret physical events about the real nature of which we know nothing except what is revealed to us by our mind.

What is remarkable in this subject-object nature of the world, and the observing consciousness, is that while all we see, imagine, scan, or weigh is constantly fluctuating, the mirror which reflects every image and every thought remains the same. The same subject-object relationship—between the world and the human observer—continues to exist even in the case of the enlightened consciousness, except with this difference: The role of consciousness, as the reality behind the phenomenal world of name and form, becomes obvious.

The panorama stretching to the last limit of the horizon and the void of the ambient sky, besides all the physical objects crowded into it, seems to be filled with an immanence, a glorious inexpressible Presence, calm, serene, and blissful, unaffected by the most violent events and upheavals. It is like the deep bed of an ocean which remains undisturbed even in the most furious storm, lashing the surface waters into a violently agitated mass of racing waves.

For the enlightened, therefore, the divine and the world of forms exist side by side without causing the least confusion. The change in depth of the observing consciousness reveals a subtle new world, a living, throbbing world of unutterable beauty, harmony, happiness, and peace.

"By each of these disciplines," says Plato in *The Republic,* "a certain organ of the soul is both purified and reanimated which is blinded and buried by studies of another kind; an organ better worth saving than ten thousand eyes, since Truth is perceived by it alone."

This is the divine eye which sees the one in many and unity in diversity. This is the divine flame, burning everywhere to light the universe of suns and earths. This transcendental organ of the truly enlightened cleaves the darkness—"avidya" —of the normal human mind to introduce a new feature in the consciousness of the observer. The phenomenal world seems no longer to be a monstrous cauldron of revolving masses and clashing forces, but the planned creation of a Cosmic Intelligence ruling every atom of the colossal host.

"Neither in wood nor in stone nor in clay is the Deity," says Shankara. "The Deity is there by virtue of the mystic feeling. Therefore, the mystic feeling is the cause." In the case of the enlightened, this "mystic feeling" denotes an enhanced awareness of the living radiance that clothes every object perceived, the omnipresent glory of God which meets the eyes of the emancipated mystic and the knower of Brahma in their daily contact with people and things.

"By the necessity of our constitution a certain enthusiasm attends the individual's consciousness of that divine presence," says Emerson. "The character and enthusiasm vary with the state of the individual, from an ecstasy and trance and prophetic inspiration—which is its rarer appearance—to the faintest glow of virtuous emotion."

There are certainly degrees of illumination. Though the target is the same for all human beings, the variety in the constitution of human bodies causes differences in the degrees of enlightenment. In some cases, the experience can even trail off into insanity. In all advanced states of enlightenment, there does occur a feeling, as Alan Watts has said, "as if everything both inside and outside is happening by itself, yet at the same time as if one is himself doing it all."

In the case of the fully enlightened, the acuity of perception of the world of forms remains entirely unimpaired. If anything, it gains in the discovery of beauty, harmony, and grace, in the perception of a richness of color and tone and a thrilling sense of identity with all creation which are all absent in a mind not granted the grace. In fact, for its proper and safe expression, esthetics and morals are the necessary attributes of a personality blessed with the spiritual sight.

"Few men can attain to this Divine seeing, because of their own incapacity and the mysteriousness of the Light in which one sees," says John Ruysbroeck. "And therefore no one will thoroughly understand the meaning of it by any learning or subtle consideration of his own; for all that may be learnt or understood in a creaturely way are foreign to, and far below, the truth which I mean."

The seeing Light, which perceives the one in many and a divine immanence permeating every object seen, is an attribute of enlightened consciousness. The world and the seeing Light combine in the enlightened in presenting a far more meaningful, a far more irenic and a far more harmonious picture of the universe.

Speaking about his own illumination, Ramana Maharshi explains: ". . . Fear of death had vanished once and for all. Absorption in the Self continued unbroken from that time on. Other thoughts might come and go like the various notes of music, but the 'I' continued like the fundamental Shruti note that underlies and blends with all the other notes. Whether the body was engaged in talking, reading or anything else, I was still centered on 'I.' Previous to that crisis, I had no clear perception of my Self and was not consciously attracted to it. . . ."

Ramana Maharshi's statements could be multiplied indefinitely. In the perennial state of ecstasy, known in India as Sahaja or Jnana Yoga, the unitive state of perception becomes a normal possession of the enlightened. Eating, drinking, sleeping, or waking, the glory of the soul, whether in the contemplation of the external universe or in introspection, is never lost. It continues to shine as if a resplendent sun of life has, forever, illuminated the interior.

Compare now this picture of the beatific state, painted by countless luminaries from the dawn of history, with the opinion aired by Richard Davidson, about the nature of mystical experience: "With the instrumentation now available, it is not only possible to evolve new states of consciousness by controlling a variety of internal parameters, but one can also help people attain states that have been known to Zen and yoga practitioners for centuries. By studying these practitioners with physiological recording techniques, we can determine what aspects of their physiology they alter to attain these states. . . ."

What answer can there be to a fantastic claim of this kind? Either the whole galaxy of the earth's greatest spiritual and intellectual prodigies—Jesus, Buddha, Socrates, Plato, Plotinus, St. Paul, Shankaracharya, Lao-Tse, Nietzsche, Bergson, Ramakrishna', Aurobindo, Whitman, Emerson, and many, many others—has been wrong or woefully deluded or there is something radically wrong and confusing with modern concepts about the beatific state that allows such an entirely erroneous and indefensible view about it to take root in the minds of high-grade intellectuals.

The outcome of this ignorance can be catastrophic in view of the fact that a spiritually enlightened higher dimension of consciousness is the evolutionary goal of mankind. Not by any manipulation of mind nor by any artificially created changes in the metabolic rhythm of the body, nor with the help of any instruments or drugs can mystical consciousness be introduced in a system which is not genetically ripe for its manifestation. It is only in men and women whose brains and nervous systems have already reached a certain stage of maturity that Yoga— or any other spiritual discipline—can have the effect of generating the biological processes that lead to illumination.

Those who have sudden, spontaneous experiences of the mystical state—and their number is legion—are organically ripe for the event and need just a stimulant or a trigger to bring on the ecstasy.

The rigorous disciplines of Yoga, the control of breath, regulation of food, sleep, and bodily activity—and concentration of mind—are all methods for the utilization of certain dormant bodily forces to cause the organic changes that predispose to mystical consciousness.

One blessed with mystical vision, even though in poverty, is a monarch within. He lives in full consciousness of the glorious Light which shines not only in his interior but in every object of the world around. The sense of identity between the inner and the outer immanence continues unbroken throughout. A shining mantle of consciousness clothes the observer and the objects observed, without in the least detracting from the precision of the sensual images. The perception of a divine Presence everywhere, creating the notion of One in Many— persistent trait of mystical experience—is an inalienable feature of enlightenment.

The modern chaotic trends of thought among the seekers after the divine are the outcome of a distorted image of mystical consciousness. The aspirants do not know exactly what they have to strive for. A clear understanding of the goal and the metamorphosis involved, with all their manifold implications, is not possible for everybody. It has never been possible in any epoch of history.

In India, a special branch of literature was created in which the metaphysical aspects of mystical experience were presented in the form of stories intelligible to the masses. The present-day exponents of various religious disciplines, not aware of the sublime goal, have largely contributed to this confusion. They prescribe the same practices and repeat the same teachings which were prevalent thousands of years ago. They fail to take into account the radical change in the environment of the practitioners and the enormous leap that their minds have taken since then. What was healthy mental food in one epoch can be downright poison in another.

With his penetrating intellect Jung foresaw this danger when he wrote: "Great as is the value of Zen Buddhism for understanding the religious transformation process, its use among western people is very problematical. The mental education necessary for Zen is lacking in the West. . . . Who would dare to take upon himself the authority for such unorthodox transformation experience, except a man who was little to be trusted, one who, maybe for pathological reasons, has too much to say for himself. . . ."

At another place Jung adds: "There could be no greater mistake for a Westerner than to take up the direct practice of Chinese yoga, for that would merely strengthen his will and consciousness against the unconscious and bring about the very effect to be avoided. The neurosis would then simply be intensified. . . . Yoga in Mayfair or on Fifth Avenue or in any other place which is on the telephone is a spiritual fake."

How far the analysis of Jung has proved correct by events is corroborated by the crowds of innocent young men and women for whom a normal, healthy life of steady physical and mental application has become impossible. Hundreds of thousands of them, drawn from Europe and America, troop into eastern countries to live in unbelievable poverty and want, unable to collect enough strength of mind to extricate themselves from the lethargy and vice to which they often fall prey.

It is high time that a halt is called to this waste of life and a correct picture of mystical consciousness—corroborated by the evidence from the past—is placed before the hungry crowds. This psychological study is of the highest importance, because the nature of the impulse that draws millions to various disciplines to gain spiritual insight is still a mystery and has to be explained.

Effective, safe, and healthy methods of self-discipline to attain to higher dimensions of consciousness—in harmony with the existing social orders and the present intellectual height of mankind—need to be devised if further damage is to be avoided. In light of this fact, any scientific study of sacred visions and mystical states of consciousness can be of immense value to all people everywhere.

V

The True Aim of Yoga[*]

In all the ancient literature of India, Yoga-adepts hold a place unequaled by any other class of men. The amount of literature on Yoga is enormous. Only a fraction of it has been translated into the languages of the West, and one of the results of this lack of sufficient information on the subject has been that the real significance of Yoga is not yet clearly understood.

Broadly speaking, all systems of Yoga in India fall into two categories, Raja Yoga and Hatha Yoga. Raja in Sanskrit denotes king, and Hatha means violence. Raja Yoga implies the kingly or easy way to self-realization and Hatha the more strenuous one. Both systems base their stand on the Vedas and the Upanishads; the main practices and disciplines are common to both.

In Hatha Yoga the breathing exercises are more strenuous,

* This chapter originally appeared in *Psychic* Magazine, January/February, 1973. 680 Beach St., San Francisco, Calif. 94109.

attended by some abnormal positions of the chin, the dia-
phragm, the tongue, and other parts of the body to prevent
expulsion or inhalation of air into the lungs in order to induce
a state of suspended breathing. This can have drastic effects
on the nervous system and the brain, and it is obvious that
such a discipline can be very dangerous. Even in India, only
those prepared to face death dare to undergo the extreme disciplines of Hatha Yoga.

It should not be thought, even for a moment, that Yoga in
these forms has provided the only channel for self-realization.
On the contrary, there is hardly any mention of Yoga in the
Vedas, the oldest written religious scripture in the world.
Even in the principal Upanishads, the fountainhead of all
philosophical systems and spiritual thought in India, there is
only a passing reference in two or three of the older ones. The
most popular scripture of India—the Bhagavad Gita—and
some of the greatest spiritual teachers recommend other disciplines for the attainment of the goal. These are Nishkama
Karma (selfless action as service to God), Bhakti (an attitude
of intense devotion to the divine power), janana (exercise of
the intellect in distinguishing the real from the false), and
Upasana (worship and other forms of religious discipline prescribed in almost all great religions of the world).

However, Yoga has its own value and importance. It com-
bines a number of disciplines in an intense course of training
with the aim of making spiritual enlightenment possible in the
span of one lifetime. In India it is told that the human soul
undergoes a long series of births and deaths, coming again and
again into this world of happening and sorrow to reap the
fruit of action done in previous lives. The cycle continues,
with the practice of religious discipline, until one succeeds in
cutting asunder the chain of cause and effect to reach the final
state of union with the all-pervading, all-knowing First Cause
of the Universe.

The most authoritative book on Raja Yoga is Patanjali's
Yoga Sutras, a highly respected work more than two thousand
years old. The authoritative books on Hatha Yoga are *Hatha*

Yoga Pradipika, Siva Samhita, and others that take their stand on the Tantras. There are hundreds of books on Tantric philosophy and Tantric modes of worship.

The Yoga expounded by Patanjali consists of eight steps or parts and is, therefore, known as Ashtanga Yoga—that is, Yoga with eight limbs. Hatha Yoga has also the same eight sections, with minor differences in detail.

The eight limbs of Yoga are: Yama, which means abstention from all kinds of evil thought and deed: Niyama, which means daily religious observances, such as purity, austerity, contentment, study of scriptures, devotion to God, etc. The third is Asana, which means posture or, in other words, the most healthy and convenient way to sit for the practice of Yoga. The fourth limb is Pranayama, which means the regulation and control of breathing. The fifth is Pratyahara, which means the subjugation of the senses to bring them within the control of the mind, a very necessary preparation for concentration. The sixth is concentration of the mind, known as Dharana. The seventh is Dhyana, which means a steady, unbroken concentration for a certain length of time or deep contemplation, and the eighth is Samadhi, which means the state of ecstatic or rapt contemplation of the inner reality.

It will thus be seen that Yoga is more comprehensive and complex than is sometimes supposed. It is not only Asana or posture, which is but a method to keep the body steady and straight when practicing meditation. The practice of various Asanas is an exercise for health, and it is incorrect to say that one who is practicing several Asanas efficiently is practicing Yoga. The correct thing would be to say that he is practicing these exercises to keep his body in a healthy and flexible condition.

The reason why such a large variety of Asanas is prescribed in the books on Hatha Yoga lies in the fact that neophytes had to sit for hours at a time in intense concentration. Some sort of an exercise was necessary for them to keep their bodies in a fit condition. The books on Raja Yoga generally leave it to the student to choose an Asana for which he has a preference. The most common are the Padamasana and Siddhasana.

Similarly, mere concentration or even concentration with Asana and Pranayama is not Yoga. There are ascetics in India who can perform all the eighty-four Asanas to perfection and continue performing them all their lives, but they never attain to enlightenment. There are also ascetics who can suspend their breathing for days so that they can be buried underground or placed in hermetically sealed chambers for days and weeks without being suffocated. But despite such drastic measures, they often awake as one awakes from a deep sleep or a swoon without experiencing the least enlargement of consciousness or gaining any insight of a transcendental nature. This is called Jada-Samadhi, which means unconscious Samadhi. It is a kind of suspended animation similar to that of bears and frogs when they hibernate during winter.

There are also ascetics in India who sit in meditative postures twenty-four hours a day. They sleep while sitting upright, and on awakening after a few hours continue their meditational practices. They live austere lives, occupying all their time with meditation or the recitation of mantras prescribed by their gurus, and continue the practice for scores of years without ever rising above the human level of consciousness or experiencing the divine.

There are ascetics in India who resort to extreme self-torture and even mutilation to assuage their burning thirst for spiritual experience. They lie with naked flesh on beds of nails or keep one of their arms constantly upraised until the limb becomes atrophied and withers to a stump. Some hang from trees with their heads downward, inhaling acrid fumes from a burning fire. Others stand on one leg for days and weeks, and there are even those who gaze fixedly at the blazing sun until their eyesight is lost.

There are also ascetics in India who smoke or eat preparations from the hemp plant (hashish and marijuana) in enormous doses, often remaining under the influence of the drug day and night. These practices have been in vogue in India for many centuries without producing a single enlightened spirit. Drug-taking hermits number hundreds of thousands and are a source of unhappiness to themselves and to others. Narcotics, hallucinogens, and intoxicants are not a help but an insuperable barrier in the path of God-realization.

Interestingly, the word "yoga" is derived from the Sanskrit root Yuj, which means to yoke or join. Yoga, therefore, implies the union of the individual soul with the universal spirit or consciousness. According to all authorities, the final state of union with the divine is extremely hard to achieve. "After many births," says the Bhagavad Gita, "the discriminating seeker attains to me, saying all this (creation) is the Lord. Such a great soul is hard to find." According to the Tantras, out of thousands who take to Hatha Yoga, hardly one succeeds.

Let us examine this difficult "union" more closely. Out of the millions who have been practicing meditative techniques of Yoga, how many have attained to enlarged consciousness in the West? How many have gained that state of beatitude and spontaneous flow of higher wisdom which from immemorial times has been associated with the success of this holy enterprise? How many have published their spiritual experiences to afford a glimpse of the transcendental to other seekers in order to inspire them and to provide guidance on the path?

In India, the number of enlightened during the last one hundred years can be counted on the fingers of one hand. In ancient days, self-revelation was the first test of the spiritually illuminated. The famous seers of the Upanishads—and even Buddha—had to adduce proofs for the authenticity of their own experiences.

The aim of Yoga, then, is to achieve the state of unity or oneness with God, Brahman, spiritual beings such as Christ and Krishna, Universal Consciousness, Atman, or Divinity . . . according to the faith and belief of the devotee.

From the recorded experiences of Christian mystics such as St. Paul, St. Francis of Assisi, St. Teresa, Dionysius the Areopagite, St. Catherine of Siena, Suso, and others, and from Sufi masters including Shamsi-Tabrez, Rumi, Abu Yazid, al-Nuri, and al-Junaid, and from the experiences of Yoga-adepts such as Kabir, Guru Nank, Shankaracharya, Ramakrishna, Ramana Maharshi to name a few, it is obvious that in the basic essentials the experience is the same.

During the ecstasy or trance, consciousness is transformed and the yogi, sufi, or mystic finds himself in direct rapport with an overwhelming Presence. This warm, living, conscious Presence spreads everywhere and occupies the whole mind and thought of the devotee; he becomes lost in contemplation and entirely oblivious to the world.

The mystical experience may center around a deified personality such as that of a saviour, prophet, or incarnation or around a shunya, void, or the image of God present in the mind of the devotee, or it may be centered on an oceanic feeling of infinite extension in a world of being that has no end. It is not merely the appearance of the vision that is of importance in mystical experience. Visions also float before the eye in half-awake conditions and in hysteria, hypnosis, insanity, and under the influence of drugs and intoxicants.

It is the *nature* of the vision—the feelings of awe and wonder excited by the spectacle that transcends everything known on earth. The enlargement of one's being, the sense of infinitude associated with the figure or the Presence and the emotions of overwhelming love, dependence, and utter surrender mark the experience and make it of paramount importance as a living contact with a state of being which does not belong to this earth.

Even a momentary contact with the divine is a stupendous experience. Some of the most famous men on earth—the greatest thinkers and the ablest writers—such as Plato, Plotinus, Parmenides, Dante, Wordsworth, and Tennyson had the experience. Emerson and many, many other renowned men and women had this singular experience thrust upon them often to their grateful amazement. Most of them had undergone no spiritual discipline, and there were even some who had no firm belief in God. For even when unexpected, the experience leaves a permanent mark on life which uplifts the individual and grants him insights into the nature of things that are not possible for those who never see beyond the veil.

The experience always has the same basic characteristics. It is incredible that so many learned men and women, both scientists and scholars, should ignore a phenomenon as widespread as mystical experience has been. The phenomenon becomes even more surprising when we observe that all great founders of religion and some of the greatest philosophers, writers, and artists were endowed with beatific vision. All of them recognized it for what it was—a fleeting glimpse of another life and another world.

Yoga signifies a momentary glimpse of ourselves, unfettered by flesh and the allure of the earth. For a short time we are invincible, eternal—immune to decay, disease, failure, and sorrow. We are but drops in an ocean of consciousness in which the stormy universe of colossal suns and planets looks like a reflection that has absolutely no effect on the unutterable calm, peace, and bliss that fill this unbounded expanse of being. We are a wonder, an enigma, a riddle; even those who have access to it some time in their lives cannot describe mystical experience in a way others can understand. For the soul belongs to another realm, another state of existence, another plane of being where our senses, mind, and intellect flounder in the dark.

Yoga also signifies the fact that this metamorphosis of consciousness is not only bone and flesh, but a thinking, feeling, knowing entity whose true nature is still hidden from the scholars of our age as it was hidden from the wise men of the past. Consciousness is something intangible to our senses and mind. "Neti, neti" (not this, not this) say the Upanishads, for it cannot be described in terms of anything perceived by our senses or apprehended by our minds.

Can you explain to yourself what or who you are? What is the nature of this thinking, knowing, feeling entity in you which is conscious of the world around it and which is never able to answer the question whence it came and where it has to go.

Material progress is a preliminary step to spiritual awakening. In every civilization of the past, when the smoke and dust of the battles and struggles for supremacy died down, the eternal questions—Who am I and what is the mystery behind this creation?—began to agitate the more intelligent and evolved individuals of the populace.

The answers furnished by wise men among the Egyptians, Babylonians, Indo-Aryans, Chinese, Persians, Greeks, and Romans are still on record, and it is obvious that it is only this restless hunger of the soul to discover itself that has prompted most of man's mental, artistic, and scientific growth. In fact, at the beginning all knowledge originated from the pressures exerted by the religious thirst in man. There is nothing so erroneous as the opinions expressed by some scholars and men of science that religious experience is a pathological condition of the brain or an invasion from the unconscious. This irresponsible attitude destroys the very foundation of the precious urge responsible for the progress of mankind.

Yoga aims to give these momentous questions answers which cannot be furnished by skeptical denials, drug use, Asanas or mantras, breathing exercises, or meditation without other moral virtues. In order to be effective, Yoga must be practiced in the fullness of all its eight limbs or branches. Everyone who aspires to the supreme experience must strive for perfection; he must begin first with the development of his personality.

"I call him alone a Brahman, that is, a spiritually-awakened person," says Buddha, "from whom lust, anger, pride, and envy have dropped off like a mustard seed from the point of a needle." Mere recitation of the well-known mantra, "Om Mani Padme Om," popular among the Buddhists in Tibet, or its rotation millions of times on prayer wheels, could not bear any fruit in one who did not follow the other teaching of Gotma the Buddha. The tragedy is that people do not often understand what "enlightenment" or "self-relaization" means. It is a colossal achievement.

According to the records available, all the men who had the genuine experience through the whole course of history do not number more than a few hundred. They are far fewer in number than the men of talent and genius in all other branches of knowledge and art, but they created the revolutions in thought which continue to affect the world to this day. The spiritual-adept or religious genius is extremely rare for this reason: "Illumination" represents a transformation of consciousness, the opening of a new channel of perception within, by which the deathless and boundless universe is opened to the vision of the soul.

Just as every atom of matter represents a unit of basic energy forming the universe, every human soul represents a drop in an infinite ocean of consciousness which has no beginning and no end. The average man, oblivious to his own divine nature and unconscious of his own majesty, lives in permanent doubt because of the limitations of the human brain. He is overwhelmed by uncertainty and sorrow at the thought of death and identifies himself with the body from the first to the last. He does not realize that he has a glorious, unbounded, eternal existence of his own.

All the systems of Yoga and all religious disciplines are designed to bring about those psychosomatic changes in the body which are essential for the metamorphosis of consciousness. A new center—presently dormant in the average man and woman —has to be activated and a more powerful stream of psychic energy must rise into the head from the base of the spine to enable human consciousness to transcend the normal limits. This is the final phase of the present evolutionary impulse in man. The cerebrospinal system of man has to undergo a radical change, enabling consciousness to attain a dimension which transcends the limits of the highest intellect. Here reason yields to intuition and revelation appears to guide the steps of humankind.

The syllable "aum" represents the music of the soul. This melody is heard only when the Divine Power Center in man is roused to activity. Then a sublime radiation floods the brain like a stream of golden nectar, lighting what was dark before. As the luster spreads, the soul is filled with an inexpressible happiness and finds itself growing in dimension, extending outward like rays from the sun. It reaches all nearby objects, then spreads to the distant boundaries, including the horizon and the visible universe. There is no confusion or distortion as happens with drugs and no loss of memory as happens in hypnosis. The intellect remains unaffected, and there is no overlapping or aberration. The inner and outer worlds stand side by side, but with one momentous difference: From a point of consciousness the soul now seems to stretch from end to end, an ineffable and intangible intelligence present everywhere.

The goal of Yoga is this union with the universe of consciousness, enabling man to understand his origin and destiny in order to shape his life and the world accordingly. It is a herculean achievement, more full of adventure, risk, and thrill than the longest voyage in outer space. This is the greatest enterprise designed by nature for the most virile and most intelligent members of the race when they attain to the zenith of material knowledge and prosperity.

It is because of the extremely arduous nature of the undertaking that Buddha prescribed celibacy and a monastic life for the aspirants. This is the Kingdom of Heaven spoken of by Christ into which only the pure of heart can enter. "I call him alone a Brahman," says Buddha, "who has gone past this difficult road, the impassable and deceptive circle of existence, who has passed through it to the other Shore, who is meditative, free from desire and doubt, and released from attachment, gaining a transhuman state of consciousness." In his knowledge of the spiritual and evolutionary needs of mankind, he must tower head and shoulders above the greatest intellects of the age.

"One who has attained to union with the divine," says an Indian sage, "will not change his position even with a king." "That state is called yoga," says the Gita, "which having obtained one does not reckon any other gain to be greater, and established in which one is not disturbed even by great sorrow." Once again Jesus addressed the people: "I am the Light of the world. No follower of mine shall wander in the dark, he shall have the light of life."

"I am a king, O Sela," Buddha said to the Brahman of that name. "I am supreme king of the Law. I exercise rule by means of doctrine—a rule which is irresistible."

"In this state, that is the last state of love," says St. John of the Cross. "The soul is like the crystal that is clear and pure; the more degrees of light it receives, the greater concentration of light there is in it. This enlightenment continues to such a degree that at last it attains a point at which the light is centered in it with such copiousness that it comes to appear to be wholly light and cannot be distinguished from the light . . . for it is enlightened to the greatest possible extent and thus appears to be light itself."

Christ and Buddha spoke but the truth. They were the Light.

True enlightenment consists of reaching beyond the highest intellects of the time to grasp and proclaim the law. There is no uncertainty and vacillation, because the truly enlightened one is as sure of his perception of the higher truths revealed to him as he is of the existence of the physical world seen with mortal eyes. This is why Buddha said that his doctrine was irresistible.

The laws revealed to the illuminati provide solutions to the evolutionary problems of humanity because it is possible to look into the future and discern the turns and twists of the *predestined* path. For this reason, the "enlightened" and the "awakened" have been and always will be the spiritual guides of mankind.

It is a historic fact that the law proclaimed by Buddha, Christ, and the Gita persisted for two thousand years and more and is still honored today by millions. After only a century of domination, however, cracks have begun to show in the façade of agnostic science.

It should also be remembered that idea, intuition, and inspiration are as much a gift from universal consciousness as are the revelations of the "enlightened." The life-energy stimulating the brain in both instances is Kundalini. The same biological center of energy in the body is responsible for both mystical experience and genius. The spiritually enlightened person is simply more evolved than the talented man of science or the gifted master of art. Nature is as consistent in the realm of mind as she is in the physical world. Stern psychosomatic laws govern the evolution of man and will remain outside human understanding until they are thoroughly demonstrated in a scientific laboratory.

The enlightened prophets and seers of all nations appeared from time to time not as the result of an accident, but under the same laws as did the men of extraordinary talent and genius. They are the creations of the collective consciousness of the race which governs the survival and the evolutionary drive of the entire mass of human beings. Unknown biological laws regulate the behavior and group instinct in ants, mice, bees, baboons, migratory birds, elephants, and other forms of life. These laws are still unknown because life remains a riddle and scientists are divided among themselves about its nature and status in the universe.

At opportune times or at critical junctures, the enlightened are vouchsafed insights into supernal laws in the same way that men of genius and talent gain knowledge of laws ruling the material world. "By making Samyama on the Inner Light, one obtains knowledge of what is subtle, hidden, or far distant," says the sage Patanjali in *Yoga Sutras*. Samyama means the state of mind in the last three phases of Ashtanga Yoga: concentration and ecstatic contemplation combined.

It has been known for thousands of years that in the higher state of consciousness hidden knowledge can pour into the mind independent of experience, education, or understanding. Oracles in ancient Rome, Greece, and Egypt were expected to prove the validity of this belief. The ability to come into occasional contact with this blissful ocean of perfect knowledge and infinite wisdom is the final achievement of Yoga. There are many stages, but so long as the final stage is not reached, one cannot be said to have been stabilized in Yoga; he still belongs to the normal class of human beings. It is only when he has gained access to superhuman levels of consciousness and is receptive to revelation that he is considered to be "illuminated."

The soul of every man and woman is capable of this prodigious leap from the human to the superhuman level of knowledge when the brain is properly attuned. In dreams, in reverie, in meditation, or while listening to music, praying, walking, or even working, the window of the soul may be thrown open. Often there is a brief glimpse of the transcendental world, but many people stand face to face with the ineffable and never understand the nature of the experience.

Yoga exercises can also be directed toward worldly objectives. There are exercises that are conducive to the health and efficiency of the mind, others that lead to psychic gifts, and still others that strengthen the will and improve the ability to deal with problems. However, no single achievement of this kind—or even several of them taken together—is Yoga.

Therefore, Yoga is a transhuman state of mind attained by means of the cumulative effect of all practices combined, carried on for years, and supplemented by grace. The window of the soul cannot be forced open. The aspirant, trying his best year after year, has to wait patiently for grace. The window must be opened from the inside. The custodians of the window, in the shape of hidden devices in the brain, know exactly when the shutters are to be opened. Thus, the ascent to the next state of consciousness is difficult to achieve.

Those who have not attained to the supreme state of Yoga and validated their experience cannot be considered to be yogis, Yoga-adepts, or enlightened. They are Yoga-practitioners or Sadhakas. The true yogi is one who has attained to the state of union with the ocean of divine consciousness—call it Brahman, Atma, God, Nirvana, Allah, Ishwara, or what you will. He must have pierced the veil and gathered knowledge not available to the intellect alone. The others can be oracles, physical trainers, acrobats, dispensers of spells and charms, mantra specialists, necromancers, miracle workers, magicians, mental healers, clairvoyants, psychics, mediums, astral travelers, occultists, and the like, but they cannot be held to be yogis or the "awakened" as long as they do not transcend the human level of consciousness and present their credentials to the world. Such people are useful in their way by meeting the needs of those who are fascinated by Yoga, the occult, or the spirit world, seekers who wish to develop psychic gifts or satisfy their curiosity about the supernatural. But they should not confuse these desires for gifts and experiences with self-knowledge, mystical experience, or union with God. Above all, they should not confuse it with the supreme experience which reveals the majesty, infinite awareness, and immortal nature of the soul.

There are hundreds of thousands of men and women in this world who are intensely attracted by the occult and the supernatural. There are also hundreds of thousands for whom the riddle of existence holds an irresistible fascination and many others who have an uncontrollable desire for occult powers and psychic gifts. The seekers of all the three categories take to Yoga, spiritualism, psychical research, occult practices, and spiritual disciplines to satisfy their respective urges. This is natural and, from their point of view, correct. But there is often confusion in the interpretation of this urge and the confusion is made worse by the professionals who specialize in these three departments.

The aim of Yoga and of every religious discipline is a fruitful, righteous life and union with God.

When successful, this is designed to lead to super-rational knowledge and a higher state of consciousness. The visionary experience, as has been confirmed by almost every mystic, sufi, and yogi of the past, proves to be a source of unspeakable happiness. It provides the seeker with unwavering strength and faith, unshakable conviction of immortality, transcendental knowledge, and a blissful union with an ocean of life, beauty, grandeur, compassion, love, peace, and calm. There is no parallel on earth.

"Men of Sattvic (pure) disposition worship the gods," says Bhagavad Gita, "those of Rajasic (worldly minded) disposition worship nature-spirits and demons, while others of Tamasic (dark or undiscerning) disposition worship disembodied souls and ghosts."

The difference between the genuine quest of the soul or God and the hunger for psychic phenomena and miracles has been clearly recognized by the illuminated from immemorial times. The practices of fortune-telling, astral projection, mental healing, witchcraft, etc., were in existence from the very beginning of culture in Sumer and Egypt more than five thousand years ago. Since then, countless men and women in all parts of the earth have tried to benefit from them in some way. Millions have tried to become proficient in these activities to win power, gain fortunes, communicate with spirits, destroy enemies, work miracles, or to prolong life and conquer death. But are there any instances to prove that they succeeded or set examples for others to follow?

The miracles attributed to Christ might have benefited a few thousand persons in his time, but what has been of lasting value to mankind is the impact of both his priceless teachings and the life he lived. The miracles he is said to have performed and those ascribed to his birth now constitute one of the main factors responsible for creating doubts about the reality of his very existence. Nothing that is not in accordance with divine law survives for long. His teachings were in accord with these laws and they survive intact. His miracles were not and their importance has ended; they are not even accepted now by the rational intellects of our time.

This situation is not peculiar to Christ alone. All the phenomena attributed to Buddha, the Yoga-adepts, the Christian mystics, or other spiritual teachers of the earth by the churches are not only rejected outright by most informed people but are also used by the skeptics as a weapon to attack the very foundation of the faiths they were intended to fortify.

Many of the miracles attributed to holy men, such as levitation and flying through the air, have not only been duplicated but surpassed by science. There is nothing in the annals of antiquity relating to the miraculous or magical performances of spiritual men that can even approach the miracles wrought by the intellect. The only miracle that has survived through the onslaught of time to stand unparalleled today is the miracle of reformation—the great revolutions in thought and conduct of generations and generations of human beings. It gives testimony to the solace and strength given to the soul, to sorrow and suffering mitigated through faith, and of hope sustaining them through darkest despair toward a glorious future. Most of these are necessary medicaments and props for the human mind to maintain its confidence and courage through the laborious evolutionary ascent. This is the one miracle which science cannot ever duplicate.

The desire to solve the riddle of existence, to reach into the dark and mysterious and look into the beyond owes its origin to the deep-seated evolutionary impulse in the human mind. By means of this urge, nature plans to draw the intellect toward the investigation of the supernatural and the numinous, ultimately leading to the discovery of the superphysical forces pervading the universe.

The main purpose is to draw the soul toward an investigation of its own mystery to answer the questions that arise perennially in the minds of almost every man and woman about the problem of their own existence. The final end in view is emancipation or awareness of the soul about itself.

It is infinite, eternal, an ocean of bliss, one with the sun, stars, and planets and yet untouched by their ceaseless motion. It is the light of the universe, free from every chain that binds the human body to earth. The aim of this evolutionary impulse is to make man aware of himself. With this sublime awareness, he will regulate his life as a rational human being free from egotism, violence, greed, ambition, and immoderate desire. The aim, therefore, of nature is that every child born on earth should have the capacity to win higher consciousness and live a glorious life aware of its immortal, divine nature within while maintaining peace and harmony with every human being without.

From the zenith of material prosperity—at which mankind now stands due to the achievements of science—the ascent toward spirituality will begin. Modern knowledge, now almost at the frontier of its survey of the physical world, has but a short distance to cover to gain knowledge of the entrance to the spiritual realm. This is the biological mechanism of evolution in every human body. It has been known and worshiped for thousands of years. The activation of this mechanism through Yoga or other religious discipline leads to biochemical changes in the composition of the psychic energy feeding the nervous system and the brain, resulting in the transformation of consciousness. This transformation is of such an extraordinary nature that the individual who has the experience in its fullness is actually lifted from the level of mortals to the sphere of gods while retaining all the noble traits and passions of man. All great prophets, founders of great religions, true mystics, sages, and seers had this divine organ active from birth, or activated it with appropriate disciplines and a righteous life.

Enlightenment, then, is a natural process ruled by biological laws as strict in their operation as the laws governing the continuance of the race. The central target of this evolution is self-awareness for the soul. The moment this happens, the cycle is complete and the soul realizes its own majestic nature. The release of the soul from the realms of desire, mind, and ego and its sense of identification with the body signifies freedom from the chains that bind it to earth. It becomes conscious of its own real nature, immortal spirit free from the sorrows and contaminations of the flesh.

This life—this thinking, feeling, knowing, being whom we think is born, grows old, and dies—is, in fact, the cream of the universe. It is a spark from a boundless ocean of fire, a ray from a living sun of unlimited dimensions, unbounded knowledge, and inexpressible bliss. It is a deathless atom from an infinite universe of consciousness. It must experience itself to know its stature in order to live in inutterable peace and bliss for the appointed span of life on earth.

This, I think, is the goal of every one of us, a goal designed by nature from which there can be no deviation except at the painful price of terrible suffering and disaster. Our evolutionary course is predetermined. Our transgressions can only delay the beatific consummation but can never change or shape it according to our choice.

This, I believe, is the purpose for which you and I are here—to realize ourselves. We must know the truth: This colossal universe of matter is but a ripple in the ocean of life to which we belong. This is the reason why every great spiritual luminary laid the greatest stress on a righteous life. This condition is not imposed by man. It is the revealed injunction from the collective consciousness of the race: it is the law imposed by nature enabling us to cross the boundary to higher consciousness.

"When the vision of the lower Samadhi is suppressed by an act of conscious control, so that there are no longer any thoughts or visions in the mind," says Patanjali in the *Yoga Sutras,* "that is the achievement of control of the thought waves of the mind . . . when this suppression of thought waves becomes continuous, the mind's flow is calm." Almost all great spiritual teachers have pointed out the dangers of succumbing to the lure of psychic powers or visionary experiences on the astral or mental plane, for these constitute entanglements for the soul as confusing and as hard to shake off as the entanglements of the earth.

"As time passes," says the Taoist master Chao Pi Ch'en, "demonic states will occur to the practiser in the forms of visions of paradise in all its majesty, with beautiful gardens and pools or of hells with frightful demons with strange and awesome heads and faces constantly changing their hideous forms. If he is unable to banish these apparitions caused by the five aggregates as well as the visions of women and girls which disturb him, he must compose his mind which must be clear within and without." Keeping the mind clear within and without is indispensable in order to behold the majesty of the soul. Buddha is even more explicit in advising the suppression of the desire for psychic gifts of a miraculous kind. The desire for visionary flights, psychic gifts, and miraculous powers implies a wish to continue under the domination of the ego, mind, and senses in order to experience on subtler planes what one experiences on earth. To perform surprising feats with invisible psychic or other cosmic forces is descending again to the plane of earth.

The aim of the evolutionary impulse, on the other hand, is to bring about a state which is the very antithesis of this. It is to bring the soul to a clear realization of its own divine nature, beyond anything associated with this world. We come to earth to know ourselves. The unique mirror of life in us which reflects the universe never reveals its own amazing substance and never reflects its own world. The whole of human evolution is designed to make us aware that we are gems clothed in flesh; this awareness is not only possible but obligatory for every human being born on the earth. It may take centuries, but every human activity and every social, political, or religious order is taking part in this mighty spiritual plan.

If properly carried out, the system described in these pages will explain the nature of man's spiritual destiny to the world of science. Man must know himself to rise above the sorrow and misery, defeat and despair, distress and distraction of this world. There is nothing that can sustain him more firmly in his earthly battles than an occasional glimpse of his own majesty and immortality hidden within him by nature.

VI

The Dangers of Partial Awareness:
Comments on Alan Watts' Autobiography

It is not difficult to see that Alan Watts was one of those intellectuals in whom the evolutionary metamorphosis is almost complete, though they know nothing about their internal physiological condition responsible for the same. This partial awareness leads to spontaneous flashes of mystical experience and intense yearning for transcendence. In such cases, the sexual-cum-evolutionary mechanism acts both ways, creating sometimes an all-consuming thirst for the beatific vision and, at the same time, an insatiable hunger for sexual experience. The condition denotes, from the evolutionary point of view, a physiologically mature system, ripe for the experience, and a highly active Kundalini pressing both on the brain and the reproductive system.

But the activity of Kundalini, when the system is not properly attuned, can be abortive and, in some cases, even morbid. In the former case, the heightened consciousness is stained with complexes, anxiety, depression, fear, and other neurotic and paranoid conditions, which alternate with elevated blissful periods, visionary experiences, or creative moods. In the latter, it manifests itself in the various hideous forms of psychosis, in the horrible depression, frenzied excitement, and wild delusions of the insane. In plain words, the same life-energy (prana) which, when pure, leads to the glorious visionary experiences of the harmonized mystic, when slightly tainted, can cause gloomy moods of tension, fear, depression, or anxiety and, when irremediably contaminated, creates the shrieking horrors of madness. What Mr. Watts ascribed to himself in his autobiography *In My Own Way*—his "wayward spirit," "addiction to nicotine and alcohol," "occasional shudders of anxiety," "interest in women," "lack of enthusiasm for physical exercise"—can apply to many highly intelligent and evolved human beings, who have either reached or are on the threshold of mystical consciousness. Their condition does not remain uniformly blissful, happy, or creative because of various environmental, psychic, or organic faults. This commonly met traumatic condition of the modern, highly intelligent, or creative mind is the result of gross neglect of evolutionary needs, and should form the most urgent field of study of science. But since modern savants are either ignorant of or apathetic toward the spiritual or, in other words, the evolutionary requirements of human beings, the world will continue to suffer till a breakthrough is achieved.

The evolutionary effort is directed to the building of a still wider dimension of consciousness on the lines experienced by mystics of all countries and times in the higher states of ecstasy. It needs a greater exercise of will power and more of self-discipline to keep a mind, working at higher levels of cognition, in constant check when up against temptation or faced with the never-ending acute problems of life. The emotional content, becoming more powerful at each step of the ascent, needs a corresponding increase in the power of self-control also. It is this disproportionate state of development between the two that is often at the root of the neurotic, discordant, restless, fear or anxiety-ridden, overambitious, unhappy, excitement-seeking, unsatisfied condition of the intellectual mind. Mental tension in all civilized countries is mounting because the life we lead and the social environment we create is anti-evolutionary. This is also the explanation for the totally unexpected and startling revolution that has occurred in the thinking of the modern youth about the validity of the present social organization which has, from the evolutionary angle, outlived its utility; it now poses a real menace to human security and progress. A decrease in the moral stamina of a people is the first symptom of degeneration. A state of constant effort and vigilance is necessary to 'avoid deterioration of the moral sense, built through centuries of civilized existence.

It is not society nor civilization that have been the cause of ethical growth. They helped in its development. The cause is the evolutionary impulse in the race. Psychologists err grievously when they ascribe control or repression of wild, natural instincts to civilization. The two are interdependent and both have their origin in Kundalini, the evolutionary force still active in human beings. Enhanced moral stamina, with a strong will and a greater degree of self-control, all together constitute a sine qua non of a blissful, enrapturing mystical consciousness, operative even in dreams. Without them we often have what we find in the case of Mr. Watts, a variable mental state, prone to visionary or mystical experience on the one side and anxiety states on the other, to relentless teasing of Cupid, addiction to nicotine, alcohol, and other drugs to ease inner tensions or palliate uneasy or even agonizing states of mind, much more acute at higher dimensions of consciousness.

If the evolutionary demand is not heeded and the present political, social, and educational systems are not reoriented to meet this need, the intellectual of the future will be a sorry creature, gifted with mystical consciousness, but so much at the mercy of abnormal mental states, awful visionary experiences, fear, tension, depression, loss of sleep, ennui, distaste for work and healthy physical exertion, with overmastering sex, that instead of being a source of happiness and peace, his life will become an unsupportable burden from the age of puberty to the end. We see this happening even now and can read the symptoms in the case of millions who, once lost to a sober and regulated life, take to wandering, drugs, promiscuity, and other pastimes, without understanding the reason for their own rebellious frame of mind. They are an enigma to themselves and to modern psychologists.

The paramount importance of all revealed scriptures has been that they drew attention to the imperative need of self-discipline and certain norms of conduct and noble mental traits, without which evolution can only lead to disaster. The theophanic conceptions were used as a peg to hang their teachings on. How in the olden days could the multitudes be persuaded to accept a morally oriented life without assigning a supernatural reason or the need for the propitiation of Divinity? In fact, the need sprang from the changes brought about in the human mind and body by the inexorable pressure of evolutionary processes. With the accelerated activity of the evolutionary-cum-reproductive mechanism, there occurs a tremendous enhancement in the production of life-energy (we call it sex-energy) or prana. When the physiological organism is in perfect condition, the sublimated energy streams into the brain, raising the consciousness to inexpressible heights of oceanic knowledge and rapture. But when the system is impure, and the pranic radiation becomes even slightly contaminated, then nature tries to adjust the situation in two ways: The radiation either still finds entry into the brain in the contaminated form, leading to anxiety, fear, tension, depression, craving for some kind of excitement or mind-altering drugs and the like. This is the "dark night of the mystic," the depressive, sterile mood of the genius and the virtuoso, or "a fit of the blues" of the extraordinarily intelligent mind. Almost all systems of yogic discipline are oriented to create a harmonized and pure condition of the body in which the risk of pranic contamination, on the awakening of the evolutionary force, is minimized. Western psychology has no explanation for this unpredictable change in moods and unhappy states of mind. The other way is by enormously increased pressure—at the other end of the evolutionary mechanism, i.e., the sexual region—resulting in irrepressible amativeness. In such cases release becomes unavoidable to overcome the maddening pressure on the brain. The dominant position very often occupied by sex in the minds of creative intellectuals and their utter capitulation before it can be readily understood from this.

What Mr. Watts expressed is the basic reality on which the ancient Tantras take their stand, namely the passions and appetites planted deep in human nature. The disciplines prescribed are aimed to combat these inherent tendencies. But even so, they cannot be and should not be suppressed altogether. Moderation, according to the Bhagavad Gita, is the key. It might have interested Mr. Watts to know that the unknown author of the famous hymn to Kundalini, entitled *Panchastavi*, has almost expressed himself in the same way when he sings in a state of perennial ecstasy: "Free from all sense of dependence, neither seeking anything from anybody nor deceiving anybody nor servile to anybody, I clothe myself in fine garments, partake of delicious foods and consort with a woman of my choice, because You, O Goddess, are blooming in my heart." The singer raises no question why the mystical experience has been thrust upon him. For according to the Tantric tradition neither extreme asceticism nor immoderate indulgence is an answer to the spiritual problem of man. The use of wine and the association of women in Tantric worship and ritual has therefore a plain reason behind it, provided the limit of moderation is not violated. Alcohol as a stimulant in depressive and fear-ridden moods and the association of a member of the fair sex, one's wife or a companion, have therefore often been a necessary element in Tantric disciplines and worship. The injunction is repeated over and over again that both are to be partaken of sparingly as an offering to the divine energy or Shakti. There are elaborate rituals to regulate the use of either.

For combating the depressive or anxiety states, often attending heightened consciousness, there are specific Yoga practices and disciplines that have to be mastered from the very start.

The prescribed icon of the goddess or other Deity, to be kept before the mind in the practice of meditation, is imagined with one of the hands upraised, making the gesture of dispelling fear, which with repeated practice can tend to create a mental barrier against fear-ridden and depressive moods. Also the cultivation of a healthy sense of detachment (Vairagya) toward the body and the world or of surrender to the divine will, prescribed in most Yoga disciplines, often serves as means to the same end.

The actual position is that the needs of the flesh and the vagaries of mind are recognized and due provision exists in these ancient, tried systems to guard against pitfalls, and make available the possibility of mystical consciousness to those leading a normal life. The severely puritanic and monastic life is as inimical to the spiritual progress of mankind as a sensuous and libidinous one. Those who, therefore, raise their finger at one who acknowledges the frailty and weakness of flesh in his excursion into the mystical province or in the quest of the Supreme Light make fools of themselves before the unfathomable mysteries of nature and try to limit the whole gigantic scheme of human evolution to the size of their own puny intellect.

A humanity with inhibited appetites and repressed desires can neither propagate nor survive. There can then exist no possibility of evolution for a totally inhibited and emasculated race. In spite of the teachings of sundry prophets and saints, the human multitudes continued to live their normal lives, trusting in the grace of God and, sometimes, even the intercession of their spiritual heroes. This was nature working to preserve the race, because the other extreme would have been worse and even suicidal. Man must learn to strive for perfection, to live a most fruitful and noble life. But he must desist from uprooting, distorting, or completely and drastically suppressing any basic urge, planted by nature, for in that lies danger to himself and the race.

Mr. Watts is to be honored and admired, like Rousseau, for his candid admissions. His frank confession should help many aspiring souls to overcome fear and depression at the thought that in their daily behavior they fall far short of the ideals they have in view and, therefore, will have to pay for their lapses with a barren outcome of their search for transcendence. "O son of Kunti," says Krishna in the Bhagavad Gita, "the excited senses of even a wise man, though he be striving, impetuously carry away his mind." The real aim of spiritual discipline is to strive for self-mastery, not total negation of basic appetites and desires, and to leave the rest into the hands of Divinity. There are so many factors that go into the development of mystical consciousness, including heredity and the social environment, that it will take scholars centuries to unearth the laws and to prescribe infallible methods for the attainment of healthy and ever-blissful states of transcendental consciousness. The instability and sharp variation in mental moods experienced by Mr. Watts can be due to a number of factors, like lack of practice in self-discipline, ignorance of some of the basic facts of Yoga and the evolutionary mechanism, adverse biological factors, use of drugs, and a defective system of education and social organization prevailing at present both in the East and West. From my point of view, his autobiography should be of incalculable value to the future investigatores in the sphere of mysticism, when the biological implications of the spiritual thirst in man are empirically established and understood. I have voiced my opinion about the probable factors responsible for the divided personality of Mr. Watts without the least idea of disparagement, but only to help in understanding other aspirants on the path.

According to Alan Watts' own views, "essentially Satori is a sudden experience, and it is often described as a 'turning over' of the mind, just as a pair of scales will suddenly turn when a sufficient amount of material has been poured into one pan to overbalance the weight in the other." This possibility is readily admitted in almost all systems of spiritual discipline and often ascribed to "grace." But what should doubtless excite the curiosity of a modern thinker, in the know of the available data on body-mind relationship, is the obvious position that this sudden insight occurs only in an extremely limited number of cases, generally in highly intelligent men and women and that in the vast majority of cases, even after rigorous and prolonged application of sundry spiritual disciplines, this instant or even gradual realization or, in other words, mystical experience, never occurs even in dreams.

What lies behind this apparently insolvable mystery? Is the grace gratuitous or the harvest of accumulated Karma? A highly gifted artist, a man of genius, a woman of exceeding beauty and grace, a great inventor, or a great military commander are all said to be gifted or blessed. Those who believe in Karma ascribe their talent or beauty or skill or intelligence to Karmic causes. But in either case, at this stage of knowledge, can we deny the fact that whether a fortuitous gift, divine grace, or the fruit of Karma, in every case there is a close link between the talent or beauty exhibited and the organic structure of the individual, even though we may not be in a position to specify all the details at present.

By what flaw in our thinking do we then isolate mystical experience—the rarest of all extraordinary mental traits—from the other exceptional categories, and persist in holding that only religious striving or grace is accountable for it? If it were so, and the organic frame did not come into the picture, why should the breath, body, and mind be the center of action in all systems of religious discipline, both in the East and West? What is then the need to control passion and desire, and why, from the earliest times, has the purity of the body and the mind always been prescribed, if Buddha-nature can exist, happily and with safety, in the words of Alan Watts, "in a dog"?

"A potter who wants to make earthware," says a well-known Chinese master, Chih I (also called Chih Che), "should first prepare proper clay that should be neither too hard nor too soft, so that it can be cast in a mold; and a lute player should first tune the strings, if he is to create melody. Likewise in the control of mind, five things should be regulated." These five things are food, sleep, body, breath, and mind. The same injunction is repeated again and again in the Bhagavad Gita. The regulation of these five things is also necessary for health, mental or physical. If this regulation is not done and the mind is not controlled, meditation can lead to deceitful, awesome visionary experiences, to serious mental disturbance or even insanity, according to Master Chih I.

"He whose cares about the phenomenal state have been appeased, who, though possessed of a body consisting of parts, is yet devoid of parts, and whose mind is free from anxiety, is accepted as a man liberated-in-life (Jeewan-Mukta)," says Shankaracharya in *Vivekachudamani* (430). It is obvious that in all ancient eastern disciplines, the extreme necessity of attuning the mind and body to the higher level of consciousness, attained with Yoga and other disciplines, has been clearly recognized. The same attunement of mind and body is necessary in the case of those who have spontaneous mystical experiences as the harvest of evolutionary matureness, brought about by genetic causes, about which we are still in the dark. Many western thinkers, overconfident of their knowledge of psychology, by placing mystical experience in the category of visionary adventure, without any relation to the organism, have been instrumental in causing rank confusion over this vital issue. They fail to see that spiritual experience represents the culmination of a regular process of biological evolution and that the ignorance and disregard of the laws governing this process is at the root of the precarious balance, or eccentricity, not only of the top-rank intellectual and the man of genius but the modern mystic also. Actually the position should be otherwise, to wit, the mystic, the intellectual, and the genius should be more harmonious, calm, and balanced, as it is often they who shine as the guiding lights of humanity.

The target of the psychophysiological evolutionary mechanism in human beings, active in every member of the race, is a perennial state of mystical consciousness, free of ups and downs, devoid of complexes, tensions, anxiety, neurosis, and fear, with a firm grip on the mind and body, on emotions, passions, and intractable lusts. Even a casual glance at any authoritative ancient work on Yoga or any religious scripture of the world would show that this is the aim before every spiritual teaching.

This state of surpassing, transhuman rapture, intended by nature to be a permanent feature of the future human consciousness, in the present state of our knowledge about this biological mechanism, can trail off into depression and fear or lead to neurosis and even insanity, because of our woeful ignorance about this vital aspect of human growth. A few more confessions such as Alan Watts', and a probe directed to the avowals of thousands of human beings who have had unmistakable experiences of the Kundalini force are perhaps necessary to put open-minded and enterprising men and women of science on the trail of what is the greatest mystery of creation still lying unsolved and even unattended before us.

VII

An Interview with Gopi Krishna: On Mystical Experience, Drugs, and the Evolutionary Processes[*]

You say there is a biological process at work in man that is responsible for his evolution, and that this same process—which you call Kundalini—is also responsible for genius as well as many forms of insanity. Just what is Kundalini?

It is a very ancient doctrine. We can trace the cult of Kundalini back to a period three thousand years before the birth of Christ. We find the first signs of it in what is called the Indus Valley civilization. From some seals and figurines discovered there, we can see that people worshiped this "mother goddess." Yoga was also practiced at that time, for we see a figure of Shiva sitting in a Yoga posture in a state of ecstasy.

When you speak of the cult of Kundalini, it sounds as though Kundalini were some form of goddess or religious leader.

* Originally appeared in *Changes* Magazine, February/March, 1973. The interviewer is Gene Kieffer.

You see, it is very difficult for us at this time to imagine the structure of the primitive or even the medieval mind. If we study medicine we find that very strange and fantastic cures were proposed for sicknesses. Spells and charms and exorcisms —and many of the diseases—were considered to be due to the evil influence of demons. In such an atmosphere any abnormal or supernormal state of the body could only be attributed to some divine power.

Naturally, Kundalini eventually came to be regarded as a goddess, as a divine energy, which started from the base of the spine and then remolded the brain to a higher state of consciousness. The methods to activate it and the results that were achieved were fairly well known. We can see them described in the ancient works, but its physiological implications were not understood.

You seem to take for granted that there is an energy which remolds the brain.

There should be nothing startling in this. We see that the human mind has been in a state of evolution for many thousand years. There is a great gulf between the intellectual of today and, say, the intellectual of Egypt in ancient times. We can see from works of art, from writings, and from other signs, that the human mind has taken a tremendous leap in a forward direction. Human thinking has become more flexible and much more comprehensive.

We have to find some sort of reason for this evolution. Modern savants are unable to find any changes in the brain or in the size of the skull, so they are not able to locate the cause of this advancement in knowledge. But if we just reflect on this point, we see that no change in the mind or consciousness is possible without a change in the brain, or even in the whole body. Every thought, every passion, every emotion has some mark on our body though it may be too slight to notice immediately. This clearly means that the advancement of man from a primitive to the present intellectual state must be attended by certain physiological changes which we are not able to locate.

So there is nothing wonderful in saying that there is a power which can transform the body and the brain of man. Already this transformation is occurring, though in an imperceptible way. It occurs even in a child when he grows from infanthood to maturity. There is always a change in his brain, so that later on his rational faculty—which is dormant when he is a child—becomes manifest. In the same way the rational faculty in man has been in a very primitive or low state in the savages, but now is in a heightened condition. The reason for this is change and transformation in the brain.

Modern researchers are not able to locate this change because the alteration occurs mainly in the nerve energy, which to the ancients was known as prana. Prana is the energy we use in thinking. Certain electrical discharges occur with any activity of the brain. These electrical disturbances vary in different states of consciousness; for instance, there is one state in sleeping and another in the waking condition. Prana is the agent which causes these changes, though it is absolutely imperceptible. Scientists only measure the electrical discharges, not the mysterious agent which causes them.

If prana is imperceptible, what makes you say that it exists?

Verification is contained in the ancient books where there is a great deal of information given about it—books as old as three thousand years. And then above all, I have experienced it myself.

In your autobiography, *Kundalini,* you talk about the awakening of a cosmic energy. Was it prana that was set into motion in your body?

Exactly. It is the psychic energy that is set in motion. How can you change the body and the brain, including the nervous system, unless there is an inner transformation? You can't transform it by any other means. It has to come from within.

What is this transformation like?

You see, the transformative processes set in motion by Kundalini correspond to the heightened metabolic processes which we see in a child. It has been rightly called a rebirth by almost all the religions of the world, including Christianity. Even Christ refers to it.

But when we read of "rebirth" in the scriptures—especially the Christian scriptures—we've always thought it was just a change in personality or a change in attitude, a sort of an awakening of our spiritual instincts.

Even the awakening of spiritual instinct needs some sort of a stimulus or a change in the brain.

Every kind of mental development needs persistent and hard work. I mean that if a man desires to become a painter, he has to be an apprentice or a student of some painter. He must learn the art and practice it every day with care, and so it is the case with every profession and every system of education. Do you think that while ordinary and trivial advancement in knowledge needs careful attention and study for years, a new consciousness can develop just by some magic or by some mantra or by some spell? Isn't it ridiculous to suppose there can be such a paradox in nature that while for smaller things we should have to study and struggle and labor for years, but for this purpose of transforming our consciousness, we should just take a leap and reach it all at once?

Well, there have been some Christian mystics, even St. Paul, who seem to have had such a transformation almost overnight. How can these be explained?

If we study their lives we will find that they were lives of dedication, of devotion, of faith, of missionary service, and of other altruistic and noble actions.

What about St. Paul?

Even in the case of St. Paul there would be such factors

operating, if we study his life carefully. From his epistles and his organizing capacity we see he was a man of exceptional talent. As I have said, this evolutionary energy is taking man step by step toward higher states of consciousness. In the course of this journey he becomes intellectual, esthetic, talented, a genius, and finally an enlightened man.

We can presume that for one who has already reached the state of genius, or of exceptional talent or of extraordinary intellectual development, there is only a step between him and the next higher state of consciousness. In such cases, universal consciousness or the vision of Divinity can occur without much labor. We see this happening even in the case of Einstein. From what he writes, it is evident that he had some sort of mystical experience.

Apart from Einstein, let us examine Dr. Maurice Bucke, Tennyson, Wordsworth, and so many other thinkers, philosophers, astronomers, poets, including Plato. Though they did not undergo any particular discipline, they had the experience, and that experience left an indelible mark on their minds. Their writings and their admissions clearly reveal this. We have to admit that mystical experience, or Cosmic Consciousness, cannot only be developed by effort, but it can also occur spontaneously. This entirely agrees with my view: that there is a "mechanism" which is called Kundalini, that is carrying all mankind toward a higher state of consciousness, and that all the prophets and mystics known to history had their "mechanism" already active from birth; and also that this mechanism is active in the case of men of genius and extraordinary intellectual talent.

You say this mechanism is called Kundalini. Is this an Indian term?

Kundalini means "coiled up," a Sanskrit term intended to designate a force which is normally latent or dormant but which, with certain exercises and disciplines, can be activated and made to act like a spring which is released.

Other writers on this subject have said that "coiled up" also refers metaphorically to a snake or serpent.

Yes, Kundalini is likened to a snake. I believe this reference to snake is very ancient, and we can trace it even to the neolithic age, because the common universal symbol which was worshiped everywhere is of a snake and sun.

The local museum here in Srinagar has dozens of ancient stone statues of various gods and goddesses, and almost in every case serpents are intertwined around them.

Yes. Yes. Now for instance if we see a representation of Lord Shiva you will see a snake around his neck, another around his hair. If you see a representation of Lord Vishnu, you will see him dancing on the head of a snake, or you will see him sitting in the lotus posture, on a snake floating in the ocean of milk. Now this ocean of milk is the nerve energy in the body which we only know as the sex-energy.

Could you elaborate on this?

The whole of our body is filled with a very fine biochemical essence which I call the biological prana. Prana has two aspects, the universal and the individual. In the individual aspect it is composed of the subtlest elements. I should say some radiation from the various elements on a subatomic level. This prana is concentrated in the sex-energy. Normally the sex energy is used for procreative purposes, but nature has designed it for evolutionary purposes also.

We are all familiar with the word sublimation—or refinement and purification. Most people believe that artistic talent, and genius to a large extent, depend on the sublimation of the sex-energy. Even psychologists like Freud and Jung ascribe it to libido. Now libido is sex-energy, life-energy in other words. So, according to the view of those who believe in Kundalini—according to the views of ancient masters—the human reproductive system functions in two ways, both as the evolutionary and the reproductive mechanism. As the evolutionary mechanism, it sends a fine stream of a very potent nerve-energy into the brain and another stream into the sexual regions, the cause of reproduction.

By the arousal of Kundalini we mean the reversal of the reproductive system and its functioning more as an evolutionary than as a reproductive mechanism.

Is that the reason many religions advocated celibacy?

There must be some cogent reason for it. You see, we are not so familiar with Kundalini and why it takes a long time for us to accept the idea is because the subject has never been seriously studied during modern times. Unless sexual energy is needed in some way for spiritual disciplines, why should any prophet or any saint or any spiritual teacher recommend celibacy as a method of reaching God?

To conserve the energy?

Yes. Which means that the energy is used. Unless the energy is used, what is the need of conserving it? It should be immaterial whether it is used for sexual acts or in any other way. Unless it has a direct effect in leading to higher states of consciousness why should any spiritual teacher advocate celibacy?

In the West, we've always associated sexual activities, at least in the past, with immorality. We had no idea that sexual energy might have had another use.

Well, sometimes this idea appears to be very comic and sometimes very tragic. I cannot say what is the frame of mind of one who calls the sexual act a sin when he owes his existence to this act.

But we've been taught, at least up until the last few decades, that this is true enough; but then it shouldn't be used for any other purpose, especially not for gratification of our sensual desires—only for the reproductive process, and that's all.

Even admitting that, is the Creator or God of such a limited intelligence that he should build man in such a way that the sexual urge is the most awful impulse in him, attended with such an intense pleasure, and then rule that he is not to touch it?

It doesn't make sense, but then in religion we were never allowed to think it should make sense.

There is a Persian poet who said, "Oh Lord, you have tied me to a plank and thrown me into a rushing torrent, and then you say, 'don't wet your clothes.' " An impossibility! To have such an image of the Creator—to ascribe such narrowmindedness and lack of vision to Him—is because of our own limited and narrow intellect.

I understand that Isaac Newton, one of history's greatest geniuses, was a celibate all of his life? How do you account for that?

You know, complete subdual of sexual desire has often been considered to be the acme of perfection in those striving for God-realization. This has been a great fallacy. In some cases of born mystics sexual desire has been absent from the very birth. The same can be the case with a genius like Newton. Since reproduction is the mandate of nature for the continuance of the race—and the propagation of the enlightened mind and genius is as necessary as propagation of the common mass of mankind, even more so, for the propagation of the last two categories of man fulfills the aim of evolution also—it is easy to infer that absence of the sexual appetite in one endowed with genius or prone to mystical experience, cannot be in harmony with either the principle of propagation or continued evolution. Therefore, it cannot be considered to be a normal or healthy state of body or mind.

In actual fact, absence of sexual desire in either of these two categories has a distinct disadvantage, since it leaves no residue of vital reproductive energy in the body to meet emergencies or crises that may occur in the psychophysiological system of the individuals concerned. Since the more highly developed and sensitive nervous systems of the individuals of these categories are more prone to crises, in the stress and storm of life, it follows that the absence of a reserve to counteract the effect of these stresses leaves them, as it were, at the mercy of the adverse conditions and forces they have to face from time to time.

The greater incidence of mental aberration in men and women of these classes is often due to this deficiency of a vital reserve to fight off pressures to ensure a sane and sober attitude of the mind, resulting from a pure and healthy condition of the potent nerve-energy that feeds the superior brain. I shall explain this more fully in my books.

Such a book will be in great demand, I'm sure, but even now more and more people are becoming interested in striving for enlightenment, and the ideal way of life to be lived is a growing topic of discussion. Diet is always mentioned, but it never causes the controversy that sex does. Could you elaborate just a bit more on this?

Considering the fact that the entire cosmos, from the atoms to the nebulae, is rigidly governed by inviolable laws, it would be irrational to suppose that some men in the past found the way to spiritual unfoldment by accident. There must exist a potentiality in the human body which, under certain conditions, materializes in illumination. We do not yet know precisely what these conditions are.

However, since spiritual development cannot but be the outcome of a natural process at work in the human body, it is the height of folly to hold that the process can be accelerated by an unnatural way of life. The restrictions and taboos on marriage, sex, diet, etc., are all man-made and have no sanction from nature. They differ from country to country and from sect to sect. For example, while the greatest emphasis is laid in some ashrams on a vegetarian diet, many of the great mystics of the West, and Sufis, as also some of the illumined sages of India—for instance Guru Nanak, the inspired founder of Sikhism—had no scruples against animal foods.

The restriction on marriage and the prejudice against women is a glaring instance to show what extent even spiritual teachers are prone to error. Can we imagine, even for an instant, that it is the decree of nature that in spiritual evolution woman should not be an equal partner to man? In such a case no evolution would be possible for the simple reason that, as Mother, a woman plays a more decisive role in the initial development and the later upbringing of the child. Is it distorted thinking, engendered by an ascetic and unnatural way of life, that led to such preposterous views? It is an irony of fate that the spiritual teachings, imparted in the ashrams, originated from men who lived the life of householders.

As is well known, the main spiritual disciplines and philosophical systems of India sprouted from the seeds contained in the Upanishads. In fact, the period when the early Upanishads were written was, from the spiritual point of view, the most productive epoch in Indian history. What is now taught and practiced in most of the ashrams is borrowed from the Upanishads. They are the fountainhead from which almost all the later spiritual luminaries of India drew their inspiration.

But, strange to say, almost all the inspired sages of the Upanishads, and they number hundreds, were married men with children, who retired to forests after fulfilling their worldly duties, sometimes accompanied by their wives, toward the closing years of their lives. One of the greatest of them, Yajnavalkya, whose name is still a household word in India, had two wives. I do not say that this was right, but what I mean to say is that there was no taboo on marriage or sex at the time when India was at the zenith of her spiritual career.

The monastic system and celibacy are later developments. It was Buddha who gave the place of precedence, in spiritual endeavor, to the monastic way of life. The monks, relieved of all worldly burdens, became the chief instruments for the dissemination of his teachings. Monasticism is not a natural way of life. If the attainment of a higher state of consciousness is in accordance with a plan of nature, can we ever imagine, knowing what strong urges she has implanted in both men and women to ensure the propagation of the race, that when about to reach the goal of transcendental state of consciousness, man is to shed all the instincts and impulses that led him to the goal? By resorting to celibacy and extreme self-denial, man would bring about his own extinction at a time when he attains to the top rung of his evolutionary ladder. It is thus clear that, viewed from the angle of common sense, the prevalent ideas about the means to be adopted and the life to be led, current in the ashrams, for the attainment of spiritual goals do not stand the scrutiny of reason. They need recasting to become universal and to meet the needs of the modern, highly sophisticated age.

As spiritual evolution is a natural process, unnatural methods can never lead to a healthy consummation. What is essential is a normal, healthy, and moderate life, free from immoderate ambitions and abnormal lusts; a life that keeps man healthy in flesh and at peace with himself and the world in his mind; a life of utility to the world and, to the extent possible, of selfless service to his fellow beings; a life, in short, which our conscience and our reason tells us we should live to derive joy and peace for ourselves, both for the spirit and the mind—and to be a source of solace and happiness for others.

Such a life helps the inner processes to gather momentum and to bring the goal nearer to the individuals who adopt it. It can never be the intention of the merciful Creator that man should castigate himself and suffer excessively to reach the goal set for him. But he has to win mastery over his animal nature, so as not to be a slave to immoderate desires and lusts. He has to struggle and battle with adverse forces to gain access to the Kingdom of Heaven, in the same way as he struggles and battles to gain victory over the forces of nature to establish a happy kingdom on the earth. The only difference is that for the former he must live a life of righteousness and, instead of dissipating his energy in sexual overindulgence or in pursuit of excessive power and wealth, to harness it for the attainment of a higher spiritual goal. The arena for this battle is the world with all its problems and difficulties.

In the West we've been taught that revelation was infallible. You've used the word God and Creator a number of times. What is your view of God? How do you describe the Creator?

Well, the intelligence behind the universe.

You take for granted there is an intelligence behind the universe?

Most surely. There would be no intelligence in us if there were no intelligence behind the universe.

But there are scientists of international reputation—for instance, the Nobel Prize biologist, Jacques Monod, in France—who claim that such an idea is nonsense, that the universe is founded on chaos, or chance.

They are correct to some extent, because they are condemning themselves. You see, an animal views the universe as a place of sun, of rain, of darkness, of light, of what it sees, but it never attempts an explanation for it. He just sees it, observes it, and reacts to it by certain instincts already implanted in him by nature. Just one step ahead is man, who sees the universe, studies it, measures the dimensions, probes the depths, calculates the heights, gives the reasons, sees regularity, punctuality, and law in it. And where do all these things come from except from his own consciousness? He is only reading his own consciousness.

An animal does not argue, does not invest the universe with law. It is man who does it. We see then two different phases of consciousness. In one the universe is just a mechanically moving something, but in the other it is a lawful and ordered creation.

Wherefrom has law and order come when it is not in the animal mind? It has come from consciousness. It has come because man has advanced one step higher in the scale of consciousness. If he were to advance another step, then what he sees is the whole universe as a manifestation of consciousness and intelligence, the same consciousness and intelligence which, in a restricted way in him, invested the universe with law and order.

Everything that you see, every calculation that you make comes from you, comes from your inmost depths. Now a material scientist may argue that, well, we have gained this by experience. Why has not the ox and the cow or the fish gained it?

Then he will again argue that, well, man's consciousness took a leap, but when we ask him, how did it take a leap, he is dumb. He knows nothing. Even Darwin had to admit that we could give no definite explanation for it except that it is a part of natural selection. So you see the whole structure of materialistic philosophy has been built on suppositions and premises, not on realities. The first reality that we come across is consciousness. The world comes later. We know first ourselves and then the world.

So, the wiser course is first to understand the knower. What modern thinkers have done is to ignore or bypass the knower and start investigation of the known, forgetting that it is the knower who is doing it.

Well, you were talking about the Creator. Is your definition of the Creator simply the sum total of the consciousness in the universe? What about the material universe?

We know nothing about the material universe except what we perceive through our senses, and modern research has shown that what we perceive by the senses is not the actual pattern of the universe. The universe is composed of an energy about which we know nothing. It is not perceptible to our senses in any way, neither to our hearing, sight, taste, smell, nor touch. So what is material energy or material force, in fact? In fact, what is matter? How can we know that matter is not ultimately a form of consciousness, or that one energy, exhibiting itself both as matter and consciousness, is not the actual substratum of the universe?

I remember what Professor Lobanov-Rostosky wrote in a letter after reading your autobiography. He said it was "the first living clinical report and detailed description of the impact of Kundalini on the physical body and thereby on the spiritual development of man, the two being clearly interlocked as a single, consecutive phenomenon." Another author described the Kundalini energy as "living, conscious electricity." Has this new consciousness given you some extraordinary insights as to how the energy behaves in the body?

Let me explain a bit. We see almost a miracle happening in the womb. We see just an invisible speck of protoplasm developing and multiplying with rapidity and dividing into countless parts, the eyes, the ears, the nose, the mouth, the teeth, the bones, the cartilages, the skin, the flesh, the hairs, and hundreds of other parts and tissues of the body. How does this happen with a precision and with a speed which the human intellect is unable to grasp? It means that some sort of intelligence beyond our comprehension—of which we are not able to find any trace except by observing its activity—is present and operating in the universe. This is the Cosmic Prana.

Now you will ask how do I correlate my experience with what happens to a developing embryo in the womb? Because I saw in myself the same operation going on after the awakening of Kundalini. All the tissues and cells, the nerves and all the fibers in my body were in a state of intense activity after awakening. I was just like a child, in whom an inner reconstruction is going on. I could watch it.

How could you watch it?

Internally, by concentrating my thought on my interior, and externally, by certain physiological symptoms.

How could you concentrate your thought on your interior?

When Kundalini is awakened and this more-potent energy goes to the brain, our consciousness at once undergoes a transformation. It then gets the capacity of not only looking upon itself but even upon the body. Some healers, we find, have amazing knowledge of the body and the organs, though they have not studied in a college. Some healers could diagnose diseases even better than physicians without having any medical training.

Some mediums can give you vivid descriptions of what is happening in their interior. Some can describe what is happening in your brain, or, in other words, the thoughts that you are thinking. Some can tell you what is happening at a distance. Now how does this occur? It is the same thing, the same Kundalini awakening the consciousness, either for a long or a short period, and investing it with certain properties and powers which are not present in the normal mind. Unless you suppose a transformation of this nature, you cannot explain all these phenomena.

You mentioned that when this transformation occurs, it can be only spasmodic, as in the case of a medium.

It can be both spasmodic and also a permanent feature of human life. It happens in this way. Some people are so constituted that this potent prana-energy goes to their brain, rarely when the body is in a suitable condition. At such times their normal personality is eclipsed and they may fall in a swoon or their breathing may become very much diminished. Their heart action may stop. They may become cold and insensible to external impressions. In that condition, then, they experience an expansion of personality. They experience contact with a higher source of intelligence and power which they, in ignorance, designated as God, thinking that this was the last stage to which a man could reach.

In some cases instead of giving an impression of consciousness, the energy only expresses itself in some psychic gift, the power to read the mind, the power to read the future, the power to project itself to a distant place and describe what is happening there; I mean to say, in different kinds of psychic talent. Or it may, as in the case of a prodigy, create amazing powers in even immature children, as for instance, the gift of

painting, of music, of playing chess, and of lightning calculation.

In some cases it appears as genius and extraordinary intellect. We are surprised how a man of such frail constitution has
such a power of expression, such a command of language, such
a store of information. It is this prana which has created this
state in him. This energy can work in so many ways when it is
aroused. We find man's evolution accelerated from the time he
became agricultural, that is from the time he learned the art
of agriculture which gave him greater leisure. Prior to this he
was a hunter, a nomad, moving from place to place. He had
hardly any leisure or time for mental development. When he
got some leisure he began to study. He began to observe the
heavens. He began to look into himself and into the objects
around him. He began to pinpoint the mind, to concentrate.
By this method slowly, slowly, he reached the present exalted
stature.

Attention or concentration of mind is the instrument by
which nature accelerates the process of evolution. All religious
systems and occult doctrines prescribe meditation in one form
or the other for gaining to higher states of consciousness or to
God. Actually this is a natural psychosomatic exercise which
has been prescribed for the advancement of man.

We find this demonstrated in a remarkable degree in the
case of geniuses and men of talent. We find that from an early
age they are always prone to concentrated and abstract states
of mind. Absorption is one of the main characteristics of genius.

A man of talent or extraordinary mental efficiency whole-
heartedly works on his problems or on his art. You can see
then he is oblivious to the world. His whole being is concentrated on what he is doing at that time. The same thing happens in a mystic. There is only a greater intensification of
attention so that he becomes totally oblivious to the outer
world.

So one consistent law regulates the evolution of mankind from
a primitive state or a state of lower intelligence to a higher one,
and that is application of the mind.

You say attention is the key, and that the mystic pinpoints his mind. On what is he fixing his attention?

On what is a painter pointing his attention? On the portrait before him or on the landscape which he is trying to paint. On what is a philosopher or a mathematician pinpointing his attention? On the problems that he is trying to solve. All this attention is outward. It is devoted to some object or to some problem outside oneself.

In mystical experience this intensity of attention is devoted to the study of our own self or of our own consciousness. You see, a strange phenomenon occurs after the awakening of Kundalini. The consciousness becomes a most intriguing, a most fascinating, and a most mysterious entity, and one is never tired of studying oneself or of concentrating on oneself.

The reason why mystics always hanker after the experience is because after the awakening of the evolutionary mechanism, consciousness attains such a state of bliss, fascination, wonder, and joy, that one is always happy to observe it for as long as possible.

But what are you observing? Is it a visionary experience?

Do you know what happens to the minds of opium-smokers? Or those who use marijuana, hashish, heroin, and other drugs, including nitrous oxide?

They have hallucinations.

And visions, which are sometimes very entrancing. But they also experience a loss of intellect and judgment. In the case of mystical experience, all normal faculties of mind are enhanced, not blunted. So there is a radical difference between drug experiences and the inner bliss to which I am referring. In this case it is not a vision or a hallucination. It is the same consciousness which is working in you. When you concentrate on yourself, what do you notice, for example? Do you see visions? Do you see horrible creatures, or quaint formations, as Aldous Huxley has described?

No, unless I've taken some drugs.

In the higher state of consciousness you can see the real world even more real. You can see the same things magnified, without any visions or strange creatures or projections. You see the same thing expanded, and you see yourself by means of this expansion, one with the creation around you—without the least loss of precision of intellect, or sight, or smell.

But your eyes are closed?

Not at all . . . open.

But your eyes are centered toward your interior.

When I am in meditation and I close my eyes I witness the same thing. I don't witness the outer world; I witness the expansion of my self. I feel myself expanding and spreading everywhere. Just myself, just the consciousness, without any images —only a globe of luminosity, full of grandeur, and light.

But nothing that can be described as an entity or a landscape?

No hallucination, except in dreams. I see dreams.

But that's when you're sleeping.

A question was asked of Ramana Maharshi: "Do you see spirits?" He said, "Yes, in my dreams." I would like to tell you something which probably is not known in the West, I mean especially to the younger generation. There is not a single mention of miracles in the Upanishads, which are the fountainhead of all metaphysical and spiritual thought of India. There is not a word in favor of miracles in the dialogues of Buddha; in fact he condemns them. Not a word about miracles in the Bhagavad Gita. Krishna condemns those who practice meditation to harm others or to gain some worldly object for themselves, or in other words miracles. Not a word about miracles in the sayings of Ramakrishna, Raman, Sri Aurobindo, nor Swami Sivananda.

Do you experience this higher state of consciousness only in your periods of meditation?

It is now a constant feature of my consciousness. I had the original awakening of Kundalini energy at the age of thirty-four.

When did it become a permanent feature?

It was variable for many years, painful, obsessive, even phantasmic. I have passed through almost all the stages of different, mediumistic, psychotic, and other types of mind; for some time I was hovering between sanity and insanity.

I was writing in many languages, some of which I never knew. I was unable to meet with people, and was in a state of depression. I have passed through these stages, and then slowly my condition stabilized, till I had the first impression that something extraordinary had happened in me in the year 1949.

After that, I fluctuated for some time due to physical reasons. I had some attacks of illness when I could not properly look after myself. Soon after, however, I became stable in this present state of consciousness. The wonder is that it is still expanding, still developing, still becoming more and more beautiful and alluring. And it is this, my own experience, which has taught me that Kundalini is at the basis of genius, insanity, neurosis, prodigies, and other extraordinary states of mind.

You say it is still changing, so you don't really know the ultimate that might be achieved.

There is no ultimate in human progress. It is unfortunate that man's ego makes him believe that there is nothing above him in mind or consciousness. Actually, he is still at a very low state of evolution. He will have to evolve for hundreds of thousands of years with all the resources which science has placed at his command. Perhaps then he may be able to come in touch with the total reality behind the universe.

Religious teaching does not stand to reason, and this is perhaps why the custodians of organized faiths do not allow reason to penetrate it, why everybody has to take their teachings in faith. I am trying to sweep away these cobwebs and to place spiritual science on a true footing, a science as logical, as consistent, and as demonstrable as any other science.

How are you going to do this?

Every altered state of consciousness has a corresponding biological change in the body. Hence mystical experience must also be reflected in the body and the brain. I am trying to devise experiments by which the action of Kundalini, or this psychosomatic force which leads to higher states of consciousness, can be measured.

There are many scientists who are working with refined electronic equipment to measure biological changes that attend psychological phenomena. Is this parallel to what you are talking about?

They do not know the cause. The cause is the reversal of the reproductive system. The cause is the activity of the reproductive system turned upward. Once they accept this proposition, even the changes in the reproductive system can confirm what I say, and these changes are not confined only to mystics. They can be observed even in the insane, even in men of genius, in mediums, and in prodigies. So it is not only in one thing that what I say will be verified, but in a number of factors and in many classes of men. So a confirmation is inevitable.

Now you have established the Kundalini Research Institute here in Kashmir, and I understand that you are proceeding with some research, especially in the ancient books.

I am trying to prove by documentary research that what I am saying about the biological reactions caused by an awakened Kundalini was already known for thousands of years and is clearly mentioned in ancient books.

If it is already in the ancient documents, why haven't the Sanskrit scholars, who have delved into them so minutely, already substantiated this?

In some cases the information is expressed in cryptic language, and in other cases it is mentioned in such a veiled way that few people have understood it.

Professor Mircea Eliade, of the University of Chicago, spent a great deal of time in India, delving into the ancient Sanskrit documents. His book, *Yoga, Immortality and Freedom*, is considered a classic. He must have come across these same passages.

Yes, he even referred to some of them—not about genius—about the sexual energy going up, but without understanding the implications. There are so many factors affecting it. One is that I had the experience myself. Another is that the destined time had come.

This is a strange word to us, because very few people take it seriously. I mean that there is such a thing as destiny.

When we look at the causal world it is rigidly bound by cause and effect. But when we reach a higher dimension of consciousness we find that the rigid walls of matter melt. Space and time lose their rigidity, and there is a mingling of the past, the present, and the future. Looking at the whole thing from this point of view, what we think about the universe—the laws, the effect and cause—is a product of our own consciousness. In our dimension of consciousness, the world is not illusory. It is real. But in the next higher state of consciousness it loses its solidity. It is because of this fact that I am persuaded to say that a law, which you can call destiny, rules everything that happens in the universe. We can say that we are both free and bound at the same time. It is a paradox, but that paradox is created by the intellect.

So destiny has decided that man should begin to understand the nature of his own existence?

If you glance backward in history, you will find that all great discoveries and all flashes of intuition came in succession at their proper time. One followed the other. We have reached the limit of intellect and already we have in our hands a dreadful weapon that is the nuclear bomb. On the other side, in the psychological realm, we are still groping in the dusk. And perhaps we have not even reached the stage where the ancient Yoga-adepts had reached in India. So it is just to balance the opposite poles that this knowledge is absolutely necessary in this age.

You mean we've raced ahead intellectually and have reached a barrier beyond which we would be foolish to go unless wisdom comes to our aid?

We have already been foolish in neglecting the spiritual side altogether during the last three centuries. The people who now take to spiritual disciplines are often not of the highest intellect. All people of talent devote themselves to various professions, to studies, to occupations, to technology, to science, to philosophy, to art, and they make their names in that.

There are very few intellectuals who devoted their attention to religion. The spiritual side has been neglected. This has been a fatal blunder. The world is threatened with a disaster and everybody is nonplussed. The men of science are condemning the politicians. Some scholars think that it is the mistake of technologists. There is a lopsided development of intellect and vested interests. There are only a few people who take a planetary view, who are able to judge that even a slight error can plunge the whole of humanity into disaster.

Then you feel that the scientific investigation of consciousness—or Kundalini—would be a very sensible approach to bringing about the balance that is necessary?

It would open a new field of investigation before science and also confer validity on spiritual experience. It will influence all the spheres of human activity and harmonize the whole of mankind. In the course of years—when large numbers of people take to these practices, and they have learned the various methods of controlling their physiological reactions—there will be a crop of supermen in the race. These men will be extraordinary from every point of view.

The usual time of the awakening of Kundalini is between the thirtieth and fortieth year. So if this is the time through which man becomes mature, then the period of enjoyment will be almost double. I am confident that when the laws about Kundalini are known, the life span of man will increase to as much as 150 years, out of which the greater part will be for his enjoyment and for the exercise of all his faculties.

These supermen will be prodigies of the highest order. They will have command of all the premier languages of the world and will be able to write in verse and prose in all of them. They will have command of all the sciences, and in that condition will be able to guide even the highest specialists. It is the intuitive flashes of these giants of intellect that will yield further clues in the investigation of the phenomena of nature.

The top-most men and women among them will be the heads of states, the greatest scientists, the mathematicians, the teachers, artists, and musicians. They will be so gifted and so talented that they will be able to guide humanity in the atomic and post-atomic age. They will have known the evolutionary target set for man. And also the best means to approach it. They will introduce such reforms and have such social and political structures as allow everyone to have a chance to a higher state of consciousness. They will agree on a one-world state. Together they will devise the overall laws for the unity and progress of mankind.

Without this the future will be very gloomy—if mankind is still ruled by patriotic dictators and distorted men of letters and science. The men and women who will guide mankind will partake of the mental characteristics of a Buddha or a Christ. That is, their aim will not be to grab power or to take undue advantage of their position, but their whole life and energy will be devoted to service.

They will take pleasure from it, and they will be very contented if they find others reaching to the same heights of consciousness.

I believe that within the next thirty years the law concerning Kundalini will be established and accepted by science, and regular institutions will be open for the practices and disciplines under competent psychologists and scientists who will study the changes that occur on awakening.

When this is done, it will be an easy task for people to practice these disciplines and gain access to higher regions of consciousness. The number may be small at first, but it will swell into hundreds and thousands in the course of a few decades.